Praise for Holly Jacobs

Just One Thing

"*Just One Thing* is an emotionally compelling page-turner. I could not put it down."

—JoAnn Ross, *New York Times* bestselling author

"This poignant story about new discoveries, hope, and love is truly unforgettable."

—*RT Book Reviews*

Carry Her Heart

"An unforgettable story of unconditional love."

—Fresh Fiction

"*Carry Her Heart* is a beautiful story of love and friendship. And, Holly Jacobs' message of love is strong and touching."

—Lesa's Book Critiques

These Three Words

ALSO BY HOLLY JACOBS

Just One Thing

Christmas in Cupid Falls

Carry Her Heart

These Three Words

HOLLY JACOBS

Montlake Romance

This is a work of fiction. Names, characters, organizations, places, events, and incidents are either products of the author's imagination or are used fictitiously.

Published by Montlake Romance, Seattle

www.apub.com

ISBN-13: 9781503949676
ISBN-10: 1503949672

Cover design by Mumtaz Mustafa

Printed in the United States of America

To Jake: This one's for you!

Sometimes the deepest love isn't discovered . . .

it's rediscovered.

Chapter One

Gray held my hand as we walked along the water's edge.

The sun slid toward the horizon, trailing a brilliant pink ripple after it, like the tail on a kite. Gray didn't say anything, but a light smile played on his lips as we walked. That was enough to let me know he was happy.

So was I.

As the sun finally perched on the water's edge, we stopped. We stood in ankle-deep water on small, round pebbles, and his arm settled lightly on my shoulders as I leaned against him. A few gulls flew overhead, crying their evening lament as water lapping against the shore provided a harmony.

I thought I heard Gray whisper my name. "Addie." I turned and I saw . . .

I opened my eyes and looked out at the peninsula across the bay.

The beach from my memory was just across the small spit of land that extended out into Lake Erie, creating this sheltered bay.

The moment felt more like a dream than a true memory.

So did my feelings for Gray.

I must have loved him once.

A rational part of me knew as much, and sometimes I thought I felt the whisper of that long-ago feeling. I'd grab for it, but it always slipped through my fingers.

I couldn't hold on to it, try as I might.

I kept seeing that moment when I'd needed him most and he'd turned away from me.

It's for the best, he'd said.

I couldn't seem to move past that moment, nor could I look back before it.

I knew that wasn't fair, but that one moment obscured all the others—the happier ones I knew we'd once had. I knew they were there. Sometimes, like today, I'd capture a glimpse of them, and I could almost believe I could get my old feelings for him back, but in the end, the feelings eluded me.

I could remember them but only in the most academic sense. It was akin to knowing there are moons around Pluto. We can't see them with our naked eyes, but we know they're there. It was like that for me. I knew we'd been happy once, but I couldn't quite believe that we could get back to the way we used to be.

And I certainly couldn't bridge the ever-widening gulf between us.

To be honest, I'd given up trying.

Sometimes, I almost ached with a need to reconnect with Gray. To find a way to touch him. Not physically, but a way to shake him and make him remember the way we used to be.

If he remembered, maybe he could remind me.

I just knew that *this* wasn't it.

The half life we'd been living wasn't how we began, and I knew that we couldn't go on this way. The pain of knowing what we once were and what we'd now become was too profound. Each day I died a little under the weight of it.

The knowledge sat heavily on me, threatening to bury me under its enormity.

I should have felt happier now, or at least felt relief that I was doing something proactive.

I fingered the crisp manila envelope on the table, but I didn't pick it up.

I let it sit there, and leaned back in my chair. It needed to be done. After months of inertia, I was pushing us forward.

Yes, at the very least looking toward the future should have given me relief from the constant weight of where Gray and I had found ourselves.

Instead, I couldn't shake the feeling that I could have done more.

That I *should* have done more.

I sat on the small second-floor deck of JoAnn's Ferncliff cottage.

The cottage was nestled between a cliff and the bay, just one of a collection of old fishing shacks that had become summer homes on Lake Erie.

I'd called the cottage home for months, and this deck had become my favorite spot. Today, the sun sat somewhere between rising and noon as the water lapped at the breakwall that separated the house from the bay.

It was flanked by other old fishing shacks. The one on the left was renovated; the one on the right . . . was not.

In the distance, I could make out Presque Isle peninsula, where Gray and I had once taken that walk. It arched gracefully out into the lake, creating the bay. Only a few boats dotted the smooth waters this morning, as if they knew that winter would be here soon and they wanted to squeeze in every last sail. Soon the boats would all be put in dry dock for winter. Then the bay would freeze over and I'd have ice-fishing shacks as my new neighbors.

I'd moved into the cottage in February, so I knew what I was in for when winter hit, but I was okay with that. The view was worth the cold and the feeling of isolation. Most of the neighbors in the handful of other cottages were summertime and weekend residents. Only a handful lived here year-round. But all of them seemed to be a tight-knit group.

I'd kept my distance.

Oh, I smiled and waved as I came home or left, but I declined invitations to cookouts and coffees. Frequently, I wished the cottage stood on its own somewhere without a neighbor in sight. When I said as much to JoAnn, she'd told me I needed neighbors as well as friends.

I knew she was wrong. What I really needed was Gray.

I felt as if I were half alive on my own. As if somehow I needed him in order to be me. At least I needed him the way he used to be. The way we used to be.

Those last days we were together, I'd felt lonelier in his company than I did alone here in JoAnn's cottage.

As if she'd come at the behest of some unspoken invitation, JoAnn called "Yoohoo" from the front door.

"Up on the deck," I called down. "Let yourself in and come up."

I tried to push away my heavy thoughts. JoAnn worried about me as if I were one of her kids. She'd taken to popping in unexpectedly. She used the fact that cell phone reception was horrible down here as an excuse for not calling first, but I knew that even if reception had been flawless, she'd have still popped in to invite me over for Sunday dinners and holidays.

I might be able to decline the neighbors' invitations, but there was no declining JoAnn.

I tried not to bristle under her concern.

A few minutes later, she came through the sliding-glass door that connected the master bedroom and the deck. She held a cup of coffee aloft. "I knew you'd have yours, so I helped myself."

She sat in the second deck chair next to the hammock.

JoAnn was my friend and technically she was my boss.

But in all the ways that mattered, she was the sister I never had.

She was a tall, lanky dynamo with black hair that wore its first few streaks of gray, chocolate-brown eyes, and a toffee-colored complexion. She'd stepped back from the business—Harbor House Furniture and Design—in order to start a family. And though she frequently complained that her brain was turning to mush because of the kids, she was having the time of her life and we both knew it.

I managed Harbor House now. JoAnn and I had talked about my buying into a partnership before . . . well, before everything that happened. She'd asked me once if I'd thought about it since I moved here. I'd shaken my head and she hadn't mentioned it since.

I nodded at her coffee cup. "*Mi casa, su casa* . . . literally."

"Thanks. I'd have called first, but the reception down here is so iffy there was a chance you wouldn't get the call," she said. "And of course, even if you did, there was a chance you wouldn't answer. So, as always, I felt it was best to act first and apologize later. I'm sorry to barge in on you and interrupt your brooding." There wasn't even the slightest bit of real apology in her expression.

"I wasn't brooding," I informed her.

She rolled her eyes and took a sip of her coffee.

"Where are the kids?" I asked, hoping to change the subject.

"I left them with Michaela down the street. I might not survive Wills' potty training. I have to do potty dances after each successful . . . er, mission. And Harmon FaceTimed me two nights ago when I was at the store because Wills had gone to the bathroom and needed a Mama potty dance. Do you know how humiliating it is to have to go into the office so you can potty dance unnoticed?"

"You love every minute of it," I reminded her.

She snorted. "Wills is addicted to a new book, *Fi Fly Flo*. He says Fiona's his new best friend and he wants to keep a flying horse in his garage, just like her. If I had Piper George's number I'd . . ."

"You'd?" I asked.

"Probably just thank her for writing such a brilliant book." She sighed. "Not only do we read it every night, but Wills then requires that I make up a dream for him, just like the character in the book gets. So, yeah, I'd thank her. But seriously, *Fi Fly Flo*? Try saying that fast."

Despite my turmoil this morning, I laughed, which I knew had been JoAnn's intent with that standup-worthy routine. "You are utterly fierce, you know that, right?"

"I can keep it up," she assured me. "Joey didn't sleep more than three hours in a row last night. He's almost eight months old. I don't think I'm ever going to sleep again."

"You love every minute of it," I said again, to which she snorted again.

Before she fell into another mommy-monologue, I saw her spot the thick manila envelope on the table. "Is that it?"

I nodded. "I'm trying to work my way up to it."

"Addie, you don't have to do anything you don't want to do. Gray's not pressuring you. I'm not pressuring you—I wouldn't have the right to even if I wanted to. You can take your time."

"I've given it almost a year—"

Jo interrupted me. "Eight months, Addie. It's only been eight months. You left right before I had Joey."

I shrugged. In my heart, our marriage died months before I moved out of our house and rented Jo's lakeside cottage. "We did a round of counseling. Well, we did a session. It was awful. The three of us sitting in silence, staring at each other. It felt like that the last few months at our house. Gray and I just staring at each other, not saying anything." I shook my head. "I live here now. Gray lives in Glenwood. I've given it time."

I hoped that if I severed our legal ties, I'd be able to get over him.

I wasn't sure it would work, but moving out of the house hadn't worked, and I didn't know what else to try.

Jo nodded. She sat quietly next to me. We stared at the bay and sipped our coffees.

Seconds gave way to minutes and finally to a solid part of an hour. My coffee cup was empty and I suspected so was JoAnn's.

Some people would have pestered me with their opinions and advice. Maybe that's the mark of a true friend—the ability to sense when all that's required is your presence.

I reached over and took JoAnn's hand in mine and squeezed it. "I should go. I'm sure he's at the office by now."

She nodded. "Okay. I'll come back later with a bottle of wine and we'll watch the sunset together."

"I've already got one chilling. You could bring the boys," I offered. Despite JoAnn's complaints, Wills and Joey were delightful. There was a comfort in seeing myself through their eyes . . . and in their eyes I was a fun surrogate aunt who could be counted on for stories, snacks, and an occasional hug.

JoAnn laughed. "I think Harmon should have some quality father-son bonding time with them."

"Poor Harmon," I said with a grin. Like JoAnn, Harmon was reveling in parenthood.

"Poor nothing," she said. "He spends all day at the hospital talking to adult human beings while I'm home potty dancing and reading the same books over and over. I can recite half a dozen by heart, you know."

In a sing-song voice she recited, "Then Fi ran up to her magical horse. 'It's time to fly!' She shouted, of course. "Fly, Flo—"

I interrupted before she recited the entire book just to prove her point. "You love it." That was my mantra whenever she vented.

She laughed. "I do. But don't tell Harmon."

I didn't need to tell him because I was sure he already knew it without either of us saying a word.

We both stood and I took one last look at the bay.

"Thank you," I told her.

She smiled. "Any time, Addie. You know that."

I did know that.

What I didn't know was what I'd have done without her these last few months.

I picked up the envelope and my cup, then followed her back through the bedroom to the stairs. I looked down and noticed I had on holey jeans and a ratty old wool sweater. In another time and place, I might have changed before heading to Gray's office, but that time had passed.

Though we both lived in Erie, Pennsylvania, my place was here now, in a renovated old fishing shack on the shore of the bay, while his was in a very proper house in the old, established Glenwood neighborhood.

JoAnn followed my gaze and gave me a nod, as if she knew what I'd been thinking and approved.

"Do you need anything else?" she asked.

I shook my head.

Rather than taking me at my word, she pulled me into a hug. "This is a new chapter for you, Adeline Frasier Grayson. You can make it anything you want."

I nodded. I didn't disagree with her pronouncement, but I saw the flaw in her logic . . . I had no idea what I wanted.

After JoAnn left, part of me wanted to take the envelope and slink back up to the balcony, but I sucked up my courage, grabbed my purse, and left.

I drove across the city of Erie. Trees were awash in the autumn colors—blazing orange and deep reds—their leaves carpeted the lawns and roads.

On tree-lined streets, if there was the tiniest breeze, the leaves fluttered down and fell like rain.

Normally I'd lose myself in the beauty of the drive along Bayfront Connector. Views of the bay peeked out intermittently from between houses and businesses that dotted its shoreline. The marina was already brimming with boats that were bundled up for the upcoming winter. Between the amphitheater and the dock, those last few non-docked boats were clearly visible on the lake for quick blinks of an eye.

I drove from the dock, up State Street to Gray's office. I pulled into an empty parking space. I tossed my giant black leather purse over my shoulder and clutched the large manila envelope in my hand as I got out of the car.

Rather than going inside I leaned against the hood of my car and stared at the modern-looking building Gray and his partner, Ash, had bought for Steel, Inc.

Their offices were on the fifth floor. I knew from experience that the views of Lake Erie were breathtaking from their windows. But I wasn't here for the views.

After today, I'd probably never need to come here again.

I could almost see the ghost images of the first day Gray had showed me this building. We'd stood on this very spot, craning our necks and looking up. Then he'd reached down and scooped me into his arms, as if I weighed next to nothing. He proclaimed he was going to carry me over the threshold.

I could almost see our reflection in the glass as he carried me toward the door. Gray was tall and kept his brown hair very short. I was on the tall side for a woman, but I'd always felt small next to Gray. My dark hair had been longer then and pulled back in a ponytail.

But mainly, in that reflection, I saw me laughing and him giving me an indulgent smile.

I saw us happy.

I thought he'd put me down once we'd entered the front doors that automatically slid open as we approached. But no. Not Gray. For a quiet man, he had a sense of the theatrical.

He'd carried me onto the elevator. I'd laughed as he'd fumbled for the button for the fifth floor. He'd joined in. His laughter was rare, but all the sweeter for it.

My hand had brushed against his hair as I held on. It had been newly cut and the stubble tickled my fingertips.

Gray had carried me past the receptionist's desk and down the hall to his office. Only then did he set me down as he kicked the door shut in one fluid motion.

Then he'd kissed me.

Today, leaning against my car remembering the faint reflections of that day, holding the envelope in one hand, I reached up with the other hand and brushed my finger against my lips, as if to check and see if that long-ago kiss had left some trace.

I found none.

There was nothing but my memory of that long-ago day in a time when we were happy and thought that nothing could ever tear us apart.

Now, I knew better.

I stood alone in a parking lot, clutching the envelope that would put us both out of our misery. I wondered what would happen to my memories as time and distance separated me from them. Would they become clearer or fade altogether?

That first day I'd whispered that I loved the building, but now I'd come to hate it.

I understood that image was part of any company, but I'd never cared about image or status or any of the things that Gray insisted were important in order for his business to continue to grow and thrive.

I only cared about him.

Even if I'd been working to put my love aside, caring about him was now a part of my DNA. I couldn't extricate it even if I tried.

I would always care about him. But caring and living with were two different things.

Caring and married were as well.

I suspected caring and loving went hand in hand, but now I knew that despite what the songs said, sometimes love wasn't enough.

I rode the glass-front elevator to the fifth floor on my own two feet today. Normally I'd face the glass, eager to watch the view of the lake come into focus as I rose. Today, I faced the elevator doors and tried to brace myself for what was coming.

When the doors slid open, I walked around the corner to the receptionist.

I didn't recognize her. The company had grown so fast that I didn't know half of the people who worked for Gray and Ash anymore. I didn't stop and sign in like the sign said. I simply walked across the marble floor toward the hall that led to the dark walnut door.

"Ma'am, you can't go down there," the new, unknown receptionist called out to me.

I could make a list of the things I couldn't do, but the one that would haunt me was that I couldn't find a way back to Gray. Or maybe I couldn't find a way to bring him back to me.

I looked at the receptionist and said, "You're wrong about that."

I marched into Gray's outer office. Here was someone I still knew.

"Mrs. Grayson," his personal assistant said by way of greeting. I'd always thought her steel-gray hair seemed at odds with her name—Missy.

She mothered Gray. She'd signed on when the company was barely off the ground and had been with him and Ash every step of the way.

So had I.

I nodded at her and kept walking toward the door to his inner office.

"Addie," she said, calling me by my first name. Maybe I was hearing things, but it sounded like she had sorrow in her voice.

Was she sorry for me?

For Gray?

Or for the pieces of our marriage that she must have noticed scattered about?

"Addie," she said again, softer this time. "He's on an important call. If you could wait—"

"They're all important calls, aren't they, Missy? Sorry," I said. "This can't wait any longer."

The receptionist was at the door. "Sorry, Missy. I tried to stop her. Ma'am, you can't go in—"

"She's Mr. Grayson's wife," Missy told the worried-looking girl, who nodded then turned and went back to her desk.

I threw open his inner office door and strode inside. Gray held up a finger, telling me to wait. *Important call*, he mouthed, a hand over the receiver, as if the important caller could hear his lips move. His eyes never left me as he continued to talk, and he smiled.

I remember when that smile could stop my heart. Gray was not a person who smiled easily. His default expression was serious . . . maybe *studious* was a better word. But today's smile didn't stop my heart; it simply annoyed me.

Missy peeked in and Gray—once again in his default expression—gave her a reassuring nod. She left, closing the door behind her.

And I waited.

I remembered decorating this office for him. I'd started a fire at home, opened my computer, and went to a popular art site. "Show me three prints you like," I said.

I thought he'd go for slick, sleek modern artists. I was surprised when he picked three prints by the same artist. Helen Allingham. They were English scenes. A cottage. Two children on a beach. A woman coming through a cottage gate.

Maybe I shouldn't have been surprised. Gray had always been a man of contradictions.

I fingered the plaid sofa that sat against the rich maple wainscoting, facing the maple bookshelves. The office, like the prints I'd bought him, screamed tradition. It was an odd choice for office décor in such a modern-looking building. But Gray was a man with traditional tastes who just happened to work in a fast-paced, high-tech industry.

I'd bought a Helen Allingham print for the house, too. I'd left it there, along with everything else when I moved out. I'd only taken my clothes, books, and a few mementos.

For months, I hadn't been able to remember any of our better moments, but that beach-walk memory, the first day at the office, and now the Helen Allingham prints were all good memories.

I'd hold on to them and try not to forget them again.

I studied Gray as he talked about orders, shipment dates, and invoices.

He needed to trim his hair. It had a tendency to curl if he let it grow out. He'd never trimmed it back in school. His wild brown curls had run amok. They'd softened his serious expression. But now that he was a bigwig at Steel, Inc., he wore his hair very short most of the time.

I could almost feel the way it had felt when I'd run my hands through it that long-ago first visit here. Prickly and rough.

I stood silently, waiting. The fact he was too busy to talk to me somehow made what I was about to do easier. It reaffirmed that I was right to be here, to be offering him a way out.

To be offering myself a way out.

Maybe if we ended things now we could avoid too much bitterness and find some sort of peace with our time together.

Gray hung up the phone and smiled again. It was a hesitant smile that said he was happy to see me, but dancing around the corners of his dark brown eyes was concern. I knew he was worried about what brought me here.

He glanced at the envelope in my hand and that smile faltered.

I was pretty sure he knew what was in the envelope, but he didn't admit to it. He simply said, "This is a surprise. What brings you here today?"

Suddenly, I couldn't find the words I'd practiced in my head.

Gray didn't push. Instead he said, "I almost called you last night."

"Why?" What could he have to say to me now when all those months I'd waited for something and he'd said nothing?

I waited for him now to respond. He paused, as if trying to remember why he'd almost called last night. Finally he admitted, "I opened the freezer, saw the ice cream, and thought of you."

This was so, well, Gray-ish that I couldn't help but smile. "I like ice cream, but I'm not sure I understand."

"I bought it the day you left."

I still didn't understand, and my expression must have said as much because Gray said, "You always said there's no such thing as a bad time for ice cream. So when you left, I bought it for when you came home. It's been waiting. At first I thought we could have it as we worked this all out. And as the days turned to weeks and then to months, I thought I'd give you the ice cream when I told you—"

I cut him off.

I'd waited months for him to say something, and now that he was about to, I wasn't sure I wanted to hear what he had to say. So rather than let him continue, I asked, "When did I say that about ice cream?"

"We were sixteen and Erie was having a record-breaking cold streak. The temperatures had been in the negatives for well over a week. We were driving down Peach Street, past the old Baskin-Robbins, and you screamed for me to stop. I thought we'd hit someone, but then you pointed to the store and said you were *dying* for ice cream. You said the word *dying* so dramatically." He chuckled as if my drama still amused him.

"I said it was too cold," he continued. "You said, *It's never too cold for it.* Then to make sure I understood, you said, *There's never a bad time for ice cream.*"

I remembered the old Baskin-Robbins and I did love ice cream, but I had to admit, "I don't remember saying that."

"I do. You got pralines and cream then teased me because I got plain vanilla. You laughed because I had all those choices and still, I just got vanilla."

He paused, then added, "I remember everything. Sometimes I worry that you've forgotten all the good things. And there were so many good things, Addie."

I knew there were, but he was right. They didn't come to mind often, today being an exception, not the norm.

When I didn't speak, he continued, "You said it again that one Thanksgiving when you burned the pumpkin pies."

This was an old argument. More of a joke than anything else. "You burned the pies," I said on cue.

"And you happened to have pumpkin pie ice cream that you served and said . . ."

"There's never a bad time for ice cream," I parroted.

Gray wasn't someone who was prone to jocularity, but he laughed.

And I felt it. For the first time in a year—I could almost hear JoAnn whisper "eight months"—I felt our old connection. Just a tenuous one, but something in me seemed to lighten as I recognized it.

I became very aware of the envelope in my hand.

"I don't know where we went wrong," he said, more musing to himself than looking for a response from me. "I had it all planned out perfectly and then it went to hell."

He seemed to collect himself and zeroed in on the manila envelope I was carrying. "Why are you here today, Addie? I suspect it wasn't to reminisce about ice cream."

Maybe that wasn't why I came here, but maybe that's exactly what I wanted. I wanted to connect with him. Maybe if we could talk about old memories and ice cream, we could finally talk about the elephant in the room. And if we could find our way around that elephant, maybe . . .

Gray walked around the desk and stood in front of me. Close. As if in slow motion, his hand bridged the space between us and brushed my jawline. "Addie, I—"

Gray grabbed at his chest and made a sound that was somewhere between a strangled scream and a moan. It was a sound that spoke of shock and pain.

"Gray?" I cried and tried to grab him as he collapsed. It was as if some unseen force had driven him to his knees. He crumpled to the ground, still moaning, and curled into a ball.

I dropped my purse and the envelope on his desk and knelt by his side.

He groaned.

I'm not sure why, but I loosened his tie and unbuttoned his shirt as I screamed, "Missy, call 911."

He moaned again.

"Gray. Please. Tell me what it is."

"Don't. Know." Each word was forced, as if his pain was a physical entity he had to push each word past.

He'd grabbed his chest. A heart attack? I'd seen television heart attacks and none seemed to be this painful.

I screamed again, "Missy!"

She showed up in the doorway. "They're on their way, Addie."

"Ad." Gray grabbed at my hand. "I lo—"

Loved me? Loathed me?

I wasn't sure which he meant.

He didn't say anything else. He lay, curled up and clutching his chest with one hand, squeezing my hand with the other.

"Love," he managed.

Love.

He loved me.

Old emotions whirled with new ones. Love with anger. Longing with loneliness. Joy with pain.

Things blurred and I had trouble following what was going on around us as I clutched his hand, as if holding on to it would keep him from leaving me.

The paramedics worked around us, but my focus was on Gray. I did register when one asked his name. That was one question I could answer. "Gray."

Then I remembered that wasn't his real name. "Graham Grayson. But he hates the name Graham. He goes by Gray."

The man nodded, as if I'd passed some test. "Any history of heart disease? High blood pressure?"

"No. I don't think so." I didn't know and I should. A wife should know things like that.

The paramedic kept barking questions. Gray's age. "Thirty."

Thirty was way too young to have a heart attack so it couldn't be a heart attack. I'd seen doctor shows where patients rush to the emergency room, sure that they're having a heart attack when all they really had was gas.

I tried to believe that this was the case, but looking at him in agony, I knew this was something worse than gas.

The paramedics began to load Gray on a gurney. He gripped my hand, or maybe I held on to his. Either way, we didn't break our connection as they lifted him.

They started moving him and as we reached the doorway, I had no choice but to let go. I turned around, grabbed my purse and the envelope from the desk. Then I noticed that Gray kept an old picture of us on his desk in the corner, right where it had always been.

It was as if for that moment, time slowed as I looked at the eighteen-year-old versions of us. That picture was taken at our high school graduation. We'd still been best friends then.

I could almost hear my mother. "For goodness' sake, Addie, move closer to him. Gray doesn't bite."

Softly, so she wouldn't hear, I said, "But he does have cooties," and

I crossed my fingers, which was the surefire way of avoiding cootie contamination, as any third grader knew.

Gray might have grown up, but he'd heard me and seen the gesture. He'd smiled.

There he was in his black suit standing next to me in my yellow sundress with my fingers crossed.

I could see the smile playing across his lips.

Later, they took pictures of us in our caps and gowns, but this one had always been his favorite.

He'd kept it on his desk since they'd moved into these offices. But the tiny black plastic swan that was sitting next to it wasn't normally there. We'd both taken them the night of our first date, but I hadn't been sure he still had his.

Yet, here it was, right next to our picture. In other circumstances, it might make me sentimental. Maybe it would later, but for now, I put the picture and the swan in my purse and time went back to its normal speed.

"Addie," Gray called. As soon as we were through the doorway, I took his hand again.

I knew the paramedics were still talking and maybe asking more questions. I was aware that they were doing things to Gray. But it was all peripheral. Like something you noticed out of the corner of your eyes, but didn't care enough about to turn and really look at.

"Ad," Gray said.

"Here I am, Gray. I'm not going anywhere." Again I was aware of the papers I clutched in my other hand, and they seemed to be heavier than they were before.

Chapter Two

When we got to the hospital, someone gently removed my hand from Gray's.

"Please," I said. I didn't want to be separated from him, but they wheeled him through a double door.

Someone—a nurse, maybe—took me to a desk where a woman asked me more questions about Gray. His mailing address and insurance information . . .

I'm not sure what I answered and what I didn't. I'm not even sure if the answers I *did* give were correct.

I worried about Gray and kept trying to fight back the memories of the last time I was in this hospital giving some clerk information like this.

"I want to see my husband."

The woman on the other side of the desk said, "Ma'am, you can have a seat in the waiting room and someone will come get you."

"He needs me," I said. For the first time in years—maybe the first time ever—Gray needed me and I didn't want to let him down.

"As soon as you can go back with him, they'll come get you. I'll go and make sure they know you're waiting," she said kindly. She came out from behind her desk and I sat in the seat she steered me to. I gripped my purse and the envelope on my lap.

I was cold, despite the wool sweater, and I couldn't seem to clear my head.

It was as if whatever was happening to Gray was affecting me, too.

The emergency room waiting area didn't smell like any other part of the hospital. There was no harsh smell of disinfectant here. It seemed to permeate every other corner of the hospital, but here it was another smell entirely. The ER waiting room smelled of sweat and fear. It smelled of waiting and pain.

Two television sets on either end of the room created a hum that provided a background to the cacophony of voices. Some voices spoke with anger. Some voices were tinged with fear. And one young mother sat rocking a blanket-covered toddler, singing some lullaby for comfort.

"Honey," said a woman's voice.

For a moment, I thought the doctors had indeed come to get me, but it wasn't a doctor. It was an elderly woman standing in front of me. She was older than the executively dressed Missy. This woman's steely gray hair was wrapped and corded onto itself in a bun. She had glasses perched on the bridge of her nose that reminded me of a librarian I had in grade school. And she wore a frumpy dress and orthopedic shoes.

She also wore a serious expression as she thrust a cup at me.

"Here." The bitter smell told me without looking down that it was coffee. "Drink it. It'll do you good," she said in such a motherly tone I felt tears well up in my eyes.

She took the seat next to me. "Who are you here for?" she asked.

"My husband."

"I'm sorry," she said. "Me, too."

"I'm sorry," I parroted back. We both knew that the words were hollow and without any real impact.

I'm sorry was probably one of the most meaningless phrases anyone ever came up with.

Being sorry never changed anything. It was a passive response to a situation.

Action. Action brought about change.

The problem was, there was no action open to me right now. Gray's situation was in the hands of the medical staff. There was nothing I could do for him but wait.

"I'm Maude," she said, as if I'd asked. As if we were sitting beside each other at an event. As if we were simply two strangers just passing time together.

She didn't wait for me to introduce myself. She said, "It's hard to wait to hear about someone you love. I keep thinking, what if Bertie doesn't make it? I've only had him for fifteen years and that's not long enough. I met him at the Piggly Wiggly in Waunakee, Wisconsin," she said.

It took me a moment to register that she'd said her husband was the reason she was here. Maude's eyes glazed over a bit as she lost herself in the memory—as if she were no longer here and now, but had magically slid back in time to Waunakee, Wisconsin, and was standing in a Piggly Wiggly grocery store.

Even the tenor of her voice changed. It was just a breath above a whisper and she spoke slowly as she continued, "We'd both been married and widowed, but I didn't know that at first. No, the first time I saw him, he was simply a man standing in the produce section looking lost. I hadn't planned on going shopping that day, but I'd had a hankering for apple crisp. I hadn't made it forever because it's no fun to cook for just one. But I stopped at the store on a whim.

"It was as if meeting Bertie was meant to be. As if we were meant to fall in love and start a new chapter of our lives together. You see, there he was, standing by the apples as if he were just waiting for me."

I watched as she came back to the present with regret. If she could, she'd have stayed at the Piggly Wiggly on that day so long ago. I could almost smell the apples and hear the shopping carts rattling in the background as she smiled shyly at the stranger . . . her Bertie.

But there was no staying in the past. The present weighed so heavily that it only allowed her that brief respite of visiting with that cherished memory.

Maude looked around the waiting room, as if hoping to see that long-ago moment. "Bertie and I, we both had lost someone, and we realized that we couldn't go back, but we could make a new start. We could start again together. We both felt the pain of losing someone we loved, but we found joy in a new beginning with each other." She leaned closer and whispered, "Fifteen years we've been together, day in and day out. I don't know what I'll do if I lose him. I'm not sure I'm strong enough to start over for a third time."

She gave a small hiccup as she made the confession. I leaned closer and hugged her even though hugging strangers wasn't something I usually did. But I realized that Maude wasn't really a stranger. I might have just met her, but I knew her because I understood her pain. I wasn't sure how I'd start over if I lost Gray.

It didn't make sense, of course, but there it was.

"You'll do what needs to be done," I told her. "That's all any of us can do . . . what needs to be done. We can't look too far ahead. Sometimes it's easier to simply put one foot in front of the other, take one step at a time, and don't think too much about what's around the next corner."

"Yes," she said. "That's all I can do. I just need to take one step at a time and not borrow trouble."

In that moment, she made her decision. Her Bertie was here, and she was trusting he'd be okay.

"I hope you have many more years together," I said.

She asked, "When did you meet your husband?"

This was an easy question to answer. I'd told the story of our meeting so many times in the past that I was pretty sure I'd lost the actual memory somewhere in the story of the memory.

"I met Gray first day of kindergarten. I remember walking to the door of the classroom. The room smelled of crayons and glue. And it was loud. I was holding my mother's hand as I looked inside. The room seemed so big and it was filled with strangers. I remember feeling so small. My mom kissed me, told me to be good, and then left. I cried as she disappeared down the hall. But Gray walked over, put his arm around me, and told me, *It's okay. I'm here.* And it was okay. He was there all through school. First as my best friend and later . . ."

Now I dipped my toes in the past—back in a time when he was my everything, just as I was his.

How simple things had been back in school. I knew who I was and I knew what I wanted.

Back then, I'd been Gray's Addie and he was all I wanted.

"They'll both be just fine," my new friend said. Maude patted my leg. "After we met at the grocery store, Bertie took me to dinner at the diner. Why don't you tell me about your first date."

I shook my head and it jostled the coffee I'd forgotten I was holding. A drop splashed on the envelope, magnifying a small portion of Gray's name. I took a sip of the now-cold coffee, ensuring that I wouldn't spill it again, and wiped my finger across the drop on his name, smudging it.

My first date with Gray wasn't something I wanted to share. On the surface, it wasn't even much of a first date, but it was the moment when a lifelong friendship changed and became something more. I'd hold on to that story. But I owed Maude a memory in return for her sharing the Piggly Wiggly, so I pulled out something else. Not a date, but one of those moments I'd almost forgotten until now.

"I can tell you about our first dance. I went to our junior prom with Chip Smuthers, and Gray took Candy Hawthorne. We all went together. Chip drove—he had some new fancy car, I don't remember the make. But I do remember it was red . . ."

❧❧❧

"You're sure it looks okay?" Gray asked for the umpteenth time.

I felt bad. I knew that he was going to be one of the only guys not wearing a tux at the prom. He tried to pretend he didn't care, but I knew he did. Even if he weren't my friend, I'd have known it.

"I think your suit says you aren't a lemming. You don't jump off a cliff because everyone else does. You're not afraid to stand out in a crowd."

He offered me a wry smile. "I don't have much choice, do I?"

Gray had worked all through high school, but unlike some of the kids with jobs, his money went toward helping his mom pay the living expenses. He couldn't spare any of it for a tux rental.

I slugged his arm in response. He didn't grin, like other guys might have, but there was a gleam in his eye that I could read almost as if he'd said the words. That gleam said that I hit like a girl.

It was a standard joke between us.

But before he could actually say the words, Chip arrived all properly tuxed. We stayed and let my mom take the obligatory pictures. Me with Chip and then me with Gray. Everyone in school knew that Gray and I were friends. Best friends. They all knew that Gray was here at my house almost as often as I was at his house.

After my mother had enough pictures to fill a coffee table book, the three of us went to Candy's, where her mother repeated the process.

Rather than go out to a restaurant for dinner, Candy's mom had offered to make us a formal meal.

She served it all grown up and proper. She used a white tablecloth with cloth napkins. She put candles in the center of the table and laid out multiple forks.

It was easy to believe we were eating in a restaurant.

Gray held a chair out for Candy and gently helped her slide it under the table. I waited for Chip to do the same for me. He simply sat down. I started to seat myself, but Gray noticed and pushed me in as well.

Mrs. Hawthorne started with shrimp cocktails, then salads, finally steaks and baked potatoes. She made us a chocolate mousse for dessert.

When we got to Chip's fancy car, Gray held the back door for Candy, while Chip simply walked to the driver's door.

Gray got my door then walked around the car and let himself in.

I turned around and said, "I could have done it."

"Normally, I'd agree. Everyday Addie is perfectly capable of getting her own door. But my mom always says that sometimes all girls like being treated like a princess. And Princess Addie deserved to have her door opened for her."

A princess is just how I felt as I walked into the school gym with Chip on one side of me and Gray on the other. Candy was on Gray's opposite side.

The prom committee had transformed the bleachers and center court of the gym into a room that Disney would be proud of. There were small white lights dripping from all over the gym ceiling. They'd hung a gauzy material between the lights and the ceiling, too. The bleachers were hidden behind some white, gauzy fabric panels. White tablecloths, white chairs. More candles and tiny lights.

The overall effect was very princess-worthy. The four of us sat together at a table at the back of the room.

The official prom theme was "A Moment Like This." Kelly Clarkson blared the song over and over through the night. After that initial impression, the rest of the night was a blur. I wasn't much of a dancer, but Chip was. Gray wasn't a dancer either, but Candy was. That meant Candy and Chip spent most of the night dancing together or with other people while Gray and I held our table.

At one point Gray looked at me and said, "You realize we're both dating people with food names."

I hadn't, but I laughed as he said the words. "Maybe our senior year, we should try for people with plant names? Fern for you, and . . ." I was running through guys in our class, trying to find a name that would fit.

"Reed," Gray supplied.

"Ew." Reed Maverick had a name that sounded made up and he was cover-model gorgeous. It wasn't so much the fact he was really good-looking that put me off, but rather the fact he knew he was good-looking and was comfortable using that gift from nature to his advantage. Fern at least was president of student council and was part of the prom committee who'd spent so much time working on making tonight a success. Fern had some sense of purpose and competence about her that Reed was lacking.

A Celine Dion song started. Chip and Candy stopped the gyrations and slow danced. Gray held out a hand. "Want to dance?"

"I dance worse than I hit," I warned him, though we'd been friends for enough years that he already knew it.

"Me, too," he said, "but I think we can both turn in a circle together."

Celine's song talked about touching and kissing, which made me feel uncomfortable wrapping my arms around Gray's neck.

He didn't seem to notice my discomfort as he pulled me into his arms.

We danced then, and maybe to the rest of the world, we were just turning circles, but something else started to turn inside me.

I didn't analyze it or try to name it. I simply reveled in its warmth and I danced with my best friend.

No matter how sweet the siren's call of the past, the present pulled me back as easily as it had Maude. I sank further into my seat in the ER waiting room, still clutching a coffee as my arm rested on my purse and the envelope that spelled the end of my marriage to Gray.

The drone of daytime television was broken by an occasional PA announcement. The smell of stale coffee that couldn't quite mask the stench of the ER waiting room.

I wanted nothing more than to fall back to that time when I turned circles on the dance floor, held in Gray's arms as Celine Dion sang. But I held myself firmly in this place. I looked at Maude. "It was our junior prom and that was our first dance. And at that moment, something started to change between Gray and me. At least for me that was the moment."

We'd been friends from the moment Gray had wrapped his arm around me in kindergarten, but that night on the dance floor, we started to become something more.

I remembered that prom and the song we'd danced to so clearly. "It's All Coming Back to Me Now." I clutched the envelope on my lap and realized that there was a sense of irony in the memory of that long-ago song.

"Honey—" my waiting-partner Maude started, but she was interrupted when a doctor came into the room.

"Mrs. Grayson?" she called.

I didn't want to go because that doctor might give me news I didn't want to hear, but my new friend reached over and squeezed my hand. That tiny bit of human connection was enough to give me the courage to set down my coffee cup, grip the envelope and my purse, and move toward the doctor.

The grim-faced doctor.

She was tiny, but had an aura of confidence about her.

"It was a heart attack, then?" I asked. I knew they could do things to remove blockages. Maybe that's what she was coming to tell me.

But I realized it wasn't that simple as the doctor shook her head. "No, ma'am. It wasn't a heart attack. It was a type A aortic dissection. In layman's terms, it's a tear in a blood vessel. We're taking Mr. Grayson up to surgery immediately. He . . ."

Then she spoke *doctor* at me. She talked about his history of high blood pressure, something I knew nothing about.

I couldn't hold on to the entirety of her explanation, but I gleaned words and phrases.

Stent.

Surgery.

Sedation.

Coma.

I began to hear full sentences again when she told me that the longer Gray survived, the better his chances were.

"His risk of death will decrease with every passing hour after the surgery," she assured me, as if that would give me comfort.

Risk of death.

Despite the fact I was still clutching the divorce papers, I couldn't process the concept of my life without Gray in it.

"Ma'am, is there someone we can call for you?" she asked me kindly.

I shook my head. I'd have to call Gray's mom, Ash, and JoAnn, but that was something I could do myself. I wouldn't have some stranger call any of them with news like this.

She nodded. "I'll send a nurse in with the consent forms."

"Consent forms?" I asked.

"As his wife, you'll need to sign the consent forms that will allow us to do the surgery."

"Surgery?"

"To put in the stents," she said gently.

"For his heart," I managed.

"Yes," she said, then turned and hurried back toward the ER, as if she didn't want to get stuck answering any more of my questions.

I didn't blame her.

Normally I was pretty quick about things, but I felt like I was thinking through cotton.

I felt dazed as I walked back across the room and sat down across from Maude.

"It doesn't sound good," I said. I needed to say the words to someone. I needed to hear what they sounded like.

It doesn't sound good.

The words were daggers. They were more painful than anything I'd heard or felt this last year.

Maude didn't say anything. She didn't try to paint a good face on it. She simply reached across the expanse that separated us and patted my hand.

The nurse came with the papers, which I duly signed. "If you'll follow me, I'll take you up to the surgical waiting room."

I nodded and stood again. "I've got to go," I told Bertie's wife. "I hope Bertie's okay."

"I'll say a prayer for your husband," she said in response.

"Thank you, Maude." I nodded.

The young nurse urged me to come along by only saying my name. "Mrs. Grayson?"

Mrs. Grayson.

When I had my lawyer draw up my divorce papers, I'd thought about going back to my maiden name. Adeline Frasier.

He'd said it wouldn't be hard to have everything changed over. He'd help me.

But in the end, I couldn't do it. I'd been Addie Grayson since I was twenty-four. Rationally, I knew that was only six years out of my thirty, but those years had set their stamp on me. I'd *been* Adeline Frasier, but I *was* Addie Grayson.

It was a difference that might not mean anything to someone else, but it meant everything to me.

I might be ready to end my marriage, but I wasn't ready to put an end to who I was.

Chapter Three

"Mrs. Grayson?" the nurse said again.

I realized I was just standing in front of Maude. I nodded at her and then turned to the nurse and said, "Yes. I'm ready."

I left the ER waiting room behind as I followed the young nurse through sterile-looking halls that smelled of antiseptic. While I was sure they used it to clean germs, I suddenly thought that its acrid smell was also used to cover the smell that they couldn't quite mask in the emergency room. Maybe they thought that patients and their families wouldn't be able to smell the fear and despair that lurked underneath the antiseptic smell.

But I could.

The nurse wove through the halls.

I knew if left to my own devices I'd never find my way back through the labyrinth. Gray had always helped me with direction. To be honest,

I was hopeless. I'd lived in Erie all my life and still navigated by landmarks rather than roads.

Gray had learned to give me directions that way. *Go to the church with the stained glass front window you love and . . .*

I blinked my eyes rapidly, trying to hold back the tears that threatened to escape.

How had I imagined I'd navigate my life without him?

The papers in my hand seemed to weigh more with each passing step. This morning I'd planned to walk away from Gray permanently, and now I wanted nothing more than to see him again.

I knew that the chasm that had widened over the last year wouldn't disappear, but I also realized that it didn't matter now. Only he mattered.

What if he didn't survive?

They'd talked about his high risk of death.

"What will I do if he dies?" I asked myself more than the nurse who was escorting me.

"We're going to do our best to see to it that doesn't happen." She'd probably said those words countless times. They came as naturally to her as saying *thank you* or *please* did to me.

We both knew that she wasn't promising me that Gray wouldn't die, only that they'd do their *best* to try to save him.

What if their best wasn't good enough?

Losing Gray would devastate me. I realized that if anyone else knew about the papers in my hand, they'd wonder at my thought, but there was a vast difference between divorce and death.

Both had a finality associated with them, but death was an absolute. With a divorce, I'd still have a chance of bumping into Gray around town. I'd read articles in the paper about Steel, Inc. and they'd mention him. They'd maybe include a picture. Friends might tell me his latest news.

If we just divorced, I'd be able to go to sleep at night knowing Gray was somewhere out in the city doing something . . . even if it wasn't with me.

But now he was somewhere in this maze of pastel-walled halls and might not ever leave them alive.

The nurse led me through a doorway into another waiting room. More televisions hung overhead, and fake potted plants punctuated the corners. I knew they weren't real because this was a windowless room in the bowels of the hospital. It was as if the staff wanted to shut away all of us who were waiting. As if they didn't want the rest of the visitors to witness our anxiety, our pain, and sometimes our grief.

"Here you go, ma'am. There are drinks here," she said, pointing to a table. "Please help yourself. It will be a couple of hours at the very least," she said gently.

"Is this one of those heart procedures where you thread a catheter through a vein? I'm sure the doctor said, but I'm having trouble—" I stopped. That about summed it up. I was *having trouble* with all of this.

I, who had a head for numbers and names—

I, who had an internal clock and calendar—

I couldn't seem to keep track of what time it was, just as I couldn't grasp the name or description of Gray's problem. His heart. That's all I could seem to cling to.

Something—not a heart attack—was wrong with his heart.

I twisted the envelope tighter.

I'd expected to go into the office, hand Gray the papers. I expected him to see the logic in the terms I'd had the lawyer insert. I was leaving him the bulk of our assets. I was honest when I acknowledged that the majority of the money for them came from Steel, Inc.

I'd thought I'd hand him the papers, he'd sign them, and I'd walk out well on my way to being divorced. That's what I expected.

Not this. Not talk of surgery and death.

"It's open-heart surgery, ma'am," the nurse said gently.

"Oh. Okay."

She reached out and patted my shoulder—this young girl who had to be freshly graduated. "Just make yourself comfortable. Someone will come find you as soon as we have any news."

"Thank you." That sense of politeness was so ingrained that the words came automatically to my lips. I wondered if they sounded as superficial to her as they did to me.

I didn't want to thank this girl who looked at me with such sympathy.

I didn't want to thank her for leading me to this room that was tucked up in the depths of the hospital, hidden away from the rest of the visitors.

I didn't want to thank her for assuring me she'd come tell me if my husband was dead.

And yet the words fell unbidden from my lips.

She didn't seem to sense my antipathy. She gave me another of her sympathetic looks. "Can I call someone for you?"

That phrase.

I'd heard that phrase before.

I'd been a freshman at college and practically crawled into the campus health department.

"It's the flu," the nurse there had proclaimed. "It's making the rounds. Can I call someone for you?"

"Gray," I said and rattled off his number.

It wasn't even fifteen minutes later that he strode into the room. "You should have called me sooner. I could have brought you here."

Normally I'd bristle and remind him for the umpteenth time that I was capable of taking care of myself. But if I tried that today, we'd both know it was a lie.

"I had them call you now," I managed.

"Better late than never," he said in that clipped, succinct way of his.

Then without waiting for a by-your-leave, he scooped me up and took me back to the dorm.

He'd skipped classes for two days to take care of me.

He'd made me tea and canned soup. He'd even let me pick the television shows.

All that was sweet, but while I couldn't remember what we'd watched or what kind of soup he'd made, I remembered that he'd been there the whole time. He'd stayed with me.

I realized the nurse was waiting for me to respond to her question about calling someone.

"No, thank you. But you're right, I should make some calls. Thank you." The words slipped out again as I turned my back on her and looked at this new room.

There were maybe half a dozen people in the waiting room. All of them waiting to hear about someone they loved.

I picked a quiet corner and took one of the hard seats.

I dug my cell phone out of my purse. As I slid my finger across the screen, I saw that Ash had called five times. I didn't bother to listen to the messages, but simply hit the callback button. I knew he'd heard about Gray's collapse.

I didn't hear it ring on my end, so Ash must have pounced on it at the first sound. "Addie, I've been going crazy," he said by way of a greeting. "Which hospital are you at? Did they tell you what's wrong? How is he?"

I thought about the doctor, then the nurse's grim expression. "It's not good, Ash," I told Gray's best friend and business partner. "Not good at all."

"I can be there in ten minutes," he said. "Just tell me where I'm going."

I imagined Ash jumping from his chair and heading toward the door as he said the words. That was Ash—a charge-in-headfirst sort of man—while Gray was more of a plotter and planner. They complemented each other in business and in their friendship.

But I couldn't handle Ash charging about here. He'd pace and fret and hound the staff. And in the end none of that would help Gray.

"No, Ash. There's nothing to do here but wait. He's in surgery for at least a few hours."

I could almost picture Ash sinking back into his chair and running his fingers through his white-blond hair, his model-handsome face contorting with concern. "He had a heart attack, then?"

"No. I forget the name, but there's a tear in a vessel near his heart. They're doing open-heart surgery. I got fuzzy on some of what the doctor said, but I think they're putting in a stent, something to keep that tear from bursting. After the surgery, he'll be in a medically induced coma for days. He won't know you're here."

"But you will," Ash said softly.

His offer was tempting. But if he came to the hospital I'd lean on him and I didn't want to lean on anyone. I'd spent the last year trying to discover how to stand on my own two feet.

I think I knew my marriage to Gray was over the moment I walked out the door to our Willow Lane house, but it had taken me all these months to learn to stand on my own enough to make it official.

No matter how easy it would be to lean on Ash, I couldn't move backward. "I'm fine," I said. It was probably the biggest lie I'd ever told. I was many things, but *fine* wasn't one of them. "I'll call you as soon as I hear anything."

"I—" I thought he was going to argue, but in the end he simply said, "Whatever you need, Addie. I mean it . . . whatever. Call me no matter what time of day or night."

"I'll call when he's out of surgery," I promised, then hung up before he could offer to come down again.

I didn't want to see Ash.

I didn't want someone I knew here, watching me break down if the worst happened.

I didn't want to admit I needed anything or anyone. I wasn't someone who asked for help or favors. I needed to think I was self-sufficient.

"Are you okay?" a man from across the room asked.

I nodded and tried to offer him a smile, but I wasn't sure it was overly convincing. Then I dialed Gray's mom, Peggy's, number. It rang and rang, then went to voice mail. I hung up, not knowing how to tell Peggy in a message to come to the hospital.

Then I remembered she was on the cruise that Gray had given her as a birthday gift. She was out of the country and had warned us she'd be turning her phone off because she wasn't wasting money on adding international minutes to her plan. But she'd promised to check her e-mail daily.

I'd just read a post this morning. She talked about the island they'd stopped at and the ladies she'd befriended.

I'd sat at my computer and realized how hurt Peggy would be to come back and find out Gray and I'd signed the divorce papers. For the last year, she'd lived her life believing we'd get back together. I'd dreaded telling her I wasn't ever moving back to Willow Lane.

But I dreaded telling her Gray was sick even more.

I e-mailed her from my phone. I wrote, "*Call me as soon as you get this, please,*" in the header. I didn't want her to be too scared, but I thought that was enough to get her attention. In the body of the e-mail I wrote, "*Gray's sick and we're at the hospital. He's . . .*" I couldn't write that he could die, but I didn't want to lie. "*He's in surgery.*"

I hoped she wouldn't call until after I'd heard something about Gray's condition.

That left JoAnn. I think I left her until last because I knew her first response would be to hurry to my side. It was a wonderful quality in a friend, but this time, I needed some time to figure things out on my own.

I dialed her number and she picked up on the second ring. "Hey, Addie. Wills, what did I say about touching the knobs on the stove? No.

I mean it. No. Or else . . ." She left the threat hanging and said, "How did Gray take it? Did he sign the papers?"

Her muffled voice said, "Wills, you are testing my patience. One. Two." She came back on. "Someday he's going to realize that three is just another number and nothing's going to happen if I get that far. So, back to you. Do you need me? I—"

"JoAnn," I said, interrupting her. "I'm at the hospital with Gray."

I could feel her still. All other thoughts faded as she focused on me with such intensity it was palpable over the phone. "What happened?"

"I went in to give him the papers." It felt like a lifetime ago that I'd marched into his office, intending to end our marriage. "He was on an important call and when he got off he told me he'd bought me ice cream and it was waiting for me. I'd been so sure this morning, but suddenly, I wasn't. Before I could make up my mind what to do, or give him the papers . . ." I still wasn't sure what I would have done.

"Before I could do anything, he collapsed. It's an aortic dissection." There, I remembered the name of it. But what it meant for Gray was still hazy. "It's some kind of tear in a vessel. They're doing open-heart surgery."

"I'll be right there," JoAnn said.

I could almost hear her starting to list what she needed to do. Find a sitter for the kids, then—

I tried to cut her off before she'd mentally restructured her whole day. "No, Jo. I'm fine. Well, not fine, but there's nothing to do but wait. I'll be here until . . ." *Until he made it or didn't.* I didn't say that part. I didn't want to talk about the chance that Gray might not make it.

I knew that JoAnn needed something to do. In a crisis, she needed to be proactive.

"Can you make sure there's coverage at the store?" I asked.

The advantage to running a small local store is we had a lot of hands-on opportunity with our clients. Our one-of-a-kind furniture, both floor models and special orders, had built up quite a following.

The disadvantage to running a small local store was there wasn't a ton of backup.

"I'll probably be here for a couple of days . . ." Maybe more.

I hoped more.

Leaving sooner would mean that Gray hadn't made it.

I pushed that thought aside. Gray would make it. He was too strong not to.

"Don't you worry about the store," she said.

JoAnn had stepped back and left the day-to-day running of the store to me when she had Wills. I had part-time help, but I shouldered most of the load. Right now, I could barely focus enough to make these few calls. Taking care of store business was beyond me.

"Wills, don't touch that," JoAnn shouted, then said, "I'll take care of everything. You stay with Gray as long as you need to. Don't worry about a thing. The store's all mine until . . ."

She let her sentence fade. She asked, "How bad is it?"

"From the looks on their faces, not good."

"Call me as soon as there's any word. As soon as he's out of surgery," she said.

"I will," I promised.

"Can I do anything else?" she asked.

Some people asked questions like that by rote, very much like I'd said *thank you*. But with JoAnn, I knew the offer was sincere.

"No, Jo, but thank you for asking." That sounded too formal for us.

She didn't seem to notice. "It's all going to be okay, Addie. You're not alone."

"I know." She was right. I'd lost both my parents, but I'd never been alone. I'd always had Gray and JoAnn.

"Thanks, Jo," I managed.

She hung up and while I knew she'd meant what she said, it didn't alter the fact that I felt alone.

Utterly and absolutely alone.

I'd done all I could do. Now all I had left to do was wait.

"You should have let someone come down and sit with you," the gentleman across the way said. "This is my wife's seventh trip to the hospital in the last year. It's easier to wait when you've got support."

Before I could say anything he gave an inelegant snort and offered me a wry smile. "I know, I'm sitting here by myself lecturing you about having support. I had people with me for the first few surgeries. When someone's got a chronic condition and requires frequent trips to the hospital, it's hard on family and friends."

I didn't ask what his wife's chronic condition was. That would have been intrusive. I simply said and truly meant, "I hope she's okay."

He nodded. "She's a strong woman. She's sweet and eternally optimistic, to the point that most people might miss that strength. But it's there."

I thought about the last time Gray and I were in this hospital. He'd been strong that time.

I wanted to just sit and not think. I didn't want to remember what we'd once had and lost.

But the gentleman in question obviously wanted to talk. "I'm James *with an S*. James Patterson." He smiled again as if it were some private joke.

He must have seen the question in my eyes because he said, "My wife is Anne with an E. Like *Anne of Green Gables*. When she says her name for someone, she always puts it that way. *I'm Anne with an E.* I started saying *I'm James with an S* to tease her."

He seemed comforted by the memory of their teasing.

"Adeline Grayson. Addie, *with an IE*," I said and smiled despite my worry. *James with an S* had given me that small smile. Until this moment I don't think I'd ever really thought about what a gift a smile was. But it was a very big gift.

But as quickly as it had appeared, it faded. I needed a moment to myself. Time to adjust to this new reality. A reality in which Gray was sick. A reality that might include a life without Gray, in a more permanent way than I'd ever intended.

James nodded, as if I'd said those words out loud as well. "I'm sorry that I'm disturbing you. It's just hard to sit here with nothing to do but worry. Sometimes I forget there was a time I wasn't worried about Anne." Softer, he added, "Sometimes I forget there was a time our lives didn't revolve around the hospital and doctors' offices. Sometimes I forget that we were once just a carefree, happy, healthy couple."

"Sometimes I forget my husband and I were . . ." Over the last few months, I'd forgotten so much. "Today, I've been reminded that we were once a happy couple." I didn't say *just a happy couple*. We'd never been *just* that. But I knew that we were happy once, just as intellectually, I knew I loved Gray once. "There was a time that I couldn't imagine my life without him in it."

I felt the weight of the papers I was still holding.

The once-pristine envelope was starting to wrinkle from all the fussing I'd done with it. I fingered the small smudge from my coffee drip earlier.

This morning when I'd taken them to Gray's office, I'd been able to picture my life without him.

I'd picked up the papers yesterday at the lawyer's office. He'd tried to tell me again that I was entitled to much more than I was asking for in a divorce settlement.

I'd told him not to worry and I'd thanked him before I walked out.

I'd stopped at 6 Mile Winery and bought a bottle of Riesling after meeting with the lawyer. It was one of my favorite new local wineries. The bottle was chilling in the fridge. I hadn't bought that wine for a celebration, but rather as a way to mark a new beginning.

A beginning of a life without Gray.

I didn't have a clue what that life would look like.

No, I did. It would look remarkably like the last year.

"When I feel overwhelmed I remember our vacation on a dude ranch in Wyoming," James was saying. "Turns out I wasn't much of a *dude*, but more of a *dud*. But Anne didn't mind. We laughed and spent the whole week together. There was nothing earth-shattering about that vacation, but it was just before she got sick. It was just the two of us and we were happy."

I could see lingering traces of that happy time in his glazed expression and before I could think better of it, I found myself sharing with him. "I had a studio apartment right out of college. It was little more than a glorified closet. But it was in one of the big, old houses downtown on West Sixth."

James nodded. Most people in Erie were familiar with that neighborhood west of the courthouse. Some of the historic homes were now businesses and many had been subdivided into apartments.

"I lived in an apartment that used to be the attic," I said. "It was a three-story walk-up."

The stairs had creaked, voicing their displeasure every time anyone in the house used them. I remembered that noise and, more than that, the smells as I walked up the flights. The people in the downstairs apartment made Italian food a lot. The entire first floor always smelled of garlic, basil, and oregano. The boys who lived in one of the second-floor units loved to party, and I think that the smell of their liquor had permeated the entire floor with a slightly sour odor.

My tiny apartment on the third floor always seemed to smell a bit musty to me, so I usually had a scented candle burning. I gravitated toward spicy scents more than floral, so I always thought my apartment smelled like fall.

I walked up those stairs in my memory. I could see some of the pocked plaster that was painted an industrial gray.

I remembered one trip up those stairs specifically. I'd carried a heavy grocery bag then. It was a paper bag, not a plastic one, or a reusable one.

"I invited Gray to supper one night," I told James with an S. "We sat on the couch and ate on the coffee table, because my apartment was too small for an actual dining room table. I made pasta—it didn't have the same heavy smells as my downstairs neighbors, maybe because it came from a jar. We drank cheap wine and spent the entire night talking about our future. I talked more than him—there's nothing unusual about that," I said. That was an understatement if ever there was one.

"I was excited about my new job. It turns out that an art degree is wonderful in theory, but not as good for getting a grown-up job. But I'd just landed a position at Harbor House Furniture and Design. I remember bubbling over with excitement."

I'd met JoAnn when I was still in school and we'd simply clicked. When she felt she could hire someone, I was thrilled that I'd get to work with her.

"There was nothing monumental about the evening," I continued. "Gray and I were just two poor, post-college kids fantasizing about a future. But I've thought about that night so many times since. I'd put candles all over the room, thinking my shabby-chic décor looked better in the dim flickering light."

I fell into the memory of that night.

Just me, Gray, and a bottle of wine then, too.

He'd talked about his business with Ash, about what he planned to accomplish. He'd been uncharacteristically an open book that night. Well, maybe just an open novella. But it was wonderful to hear him dream. Maybe that's why the evening was so easy to remember.

I'd bubbled over about my new job with JoAnn as we sat and drank in the candlelight. I wasn't exactly tipsy, but I could feel the warmth of the wine. Or maybe it was simply a warmth that came from Gray. When I'd wound down about Harbor House, he'd wound up, talking about Steel, Inc., and shared so freely. Even at that, he wasn't actually loquacious by others' standards, but for Gray, he was practically gabby.

He talked about his business plans with Ash. Big plans. Grand plans.

I had no doubt that they'd accomplish all of them.

"Once the business is secure, I'll ask you to marry me," he said out of the blue in the midst of his talk of business plans.

"Pardon?" I was pretty sure I'd heard him right, but I couldn't be positive.

"When the business is on an even keel, I'll ask you to marry me."

This time I was ready for the words.

Yes, I had heard him right. I didn't need to think about the enormity of his statement. I didn't have to weigh my response. "When you ask me, I'll say yes," I'd told him. "Whenever you ask, I'll say yes."

I couldn't stop smiling. Mrs. Graham Grayson.

No, I'd never be that.

Addie Grayson. Yes, that had a ring to it.

"So we're pre-engaged," I teased.

Gray nodded, as serious as ever. "Yes."

I was suddenly caught up in a fantasy of what our lives would look like. "When we get married, we'll buy a house up in Glenwood. One of those old brick houses where so many generations of other families lived their lives that the house has a soul, if you know what I mean."

Gray smiled then and shook his head. "I rarely know exactly what you mean, Addie."

I laughed. "Mystery is just part of my many charms. I'll decorate the house, now that I'm well on my way to making my name in design."

"You just got hired," he said in that logical way of his.

"Every designer starts somewhere. And I'm on my way. I'll decorate our house and then we'll fill it with children. Probably five."

He looked slightly panicked.

"Maybe just three," I said to reassure him. He still looked skeptical so I said, "Two. One for me, one for you. And we'll all live happily ever after."

"I want kids with you. Not right away, but when we're financially settled. When my business is a success."

I took his hand in mine and said, "I don't need you to be a success in order to marry you or build a family with you, you know. That was a lot of yous, *but you know what I mean."*

He nodded. "But I need me to be a success," he said with utter certainty. "I need to be sure I can support you."

I knew that his father had left his mom when Gray was little. Peggy worked as a waitress to support them both. Sometimes money was tight, but Peggy always managed. But I knew just eking out a living would never suit Gray. He wasn't mistaken—he didn't just want to be able to support me. He needed to.

"I can support myself," I reminded him softly.

He shook his head. "When the business is secure, I'll ask, and then we'll find that house and someday think about those kids."

Knowing that arguing with him was useless I simply smiled and said again, "And I'll say yes."

He was still serious.

"This is where you smile with relief and thank me for the reassurance," I teased him.

That did it. He'd shot me one of his infrequent smiles. "It is *a relief." He paused a moment, then he added, "I don't know what I'd do without you."*

"I know for a fact you'd never eat ice cream before dinner if I wasn't around," I teased.

"I don't do that even with you around. You do that. And sometimes, you eat ice cream before breakfast."

"Nope," I teased. "Sometimes for *breakfast. I mean, it's a dairy product, after all. And if it's strawberry, it's like eating fruit and cream for breakfast."*

Gray laughed then.

I could almost hear the sound of his laughter across the span of years. Even then I'd realized how rare it was and I'd treasured it.

I couldn't remember the last time Gray had laughed.

I thought about the ice cream that was in the freezer, just waiting for me to come home.

I looked at *James with an S*. "My husband said that someday he'd ask me to marry him at a dinner in that apartment."

"And he did," he said, looking at my hand. I looked down and was shocked to see that I was clutching the papers in my left hand, which left my engagement ring and wedding band exposed.

I nodded. "He did."

"Anne is forever showing me big-production proposals on *YouTube*," James said. "I didn't do anything like that. I took her out to dinner and slid the ring box to her. She'd picked it out, so even that was no surprise. But I asked, 'Will you marry me, Anne?' and she said yes. There was no big dance number, and no band or balloons involved. Just me and her—that was enough for me. Just her and me. That was more than enough then and it's more than enough now."

James got quiet.

I hoped that whatever was wrong with his Anne was fixable. I hoped that after all the hospital visits, this surgery would resolve her problem and allow them to still have more time together, just James and Anne.

Like Maude and Bertie.

James was lost somewhere in the past where he and Anne were simply enjoying just being the two of them.

I'd thought I wanted silence, but it weighed on me despite the fact the room was anything but quiet.

The television droned.

People conversed quietly, as if they were in a church where whispers were the norm.

They twitched and paced and talked on cell phones.

Occasional announcements over the PA system interrupted all the noise. Afterward, for half a breath the room would remain still and silent, then everything would spring back to life and begin again.

I thought I'd be thankful for the peace, but I wasn't.

I checked my phone to see if there was an e-mail from Peggy. There wasn't. Unable to sit any longer, I got up and got a cup of coffee. Thinking of Maude bringing me a cup earlier, I got one for James as well.

I handed it to him. He took it automatically, then looked down as if surprised to find coffee in his hand.

He smiled his thanks and then went back to whatever memory he'd been reliving.

I sat back down and tried to simply be still, but I felt as if I were suffocating under the weight of all that silent despair.

I picked up the conversation with James where we'd left it. "I don't think most women want a big production."

He fell back into the present and said, "Pardon?"

"You said your wife showed you big-production proposals online, but I don't think most of us want that sort of thing. I think most of us treasure the small things. We value feeling that we matter. We want to be heard. To be noticed. If you did that for Anne, it was enough."

"I keep thinking about doing some *YouTube*-worthy something for her when she's better. Something to make her smile. She deserves a big produc—"

"Mr. Patterson?" a man in scrubs called.

I felt the entire room's attention pivot to that doorway. The man said again, "Mr. Patterson."

Everyone but James went back to their conversations, television watching, or forays into their private thoughts while James stood up and took a step toward the doorway.

"I hope she's okay," I told him.

He stopped, leaned down, took my hand, and gave it a squeeze. "Me, too."

I watched as the man in scrubs said something. James listened intently, then turned back to me and smiled as he gave me a small nod.

His Anne was okay . . . at least for now.

After he left, I sat back and listened as snatches of the quiet conversations and the television drone blended together.

". . . and then she said . . ."

". . . I'd rather have my man wear nothing . . ."

". . . in for a penny . . ."

I sat and focused on the weird bits of conversations blended into an odd monologue.

". . . put the fast in breakfast by using . . ."

". . . sneakers and sweats. I said, no . . ."

". . . one memory I can't shake . . ."

Listening to the snatches of television mixing with conversations might be easier than thinking about Gray, but it kept bringing me back to him anyway.

Everything kept bringing me back to him.

I couldn't help but think about our past and trying to figure out where we went wrong.

In the months since I walked out the door, I'd figured out many things, but never that.

Chapter Four

Waiting.

Now that James had left, it felt like he'd taken what little oxygen had been in the room along with him. The weight of the waiting threatened to suffocate me.

I wondered if that's where the word *waiting* came from . . . the *weight* of the experience.

I'd waited for Gray in the past.

Waited for him to feel financially stable enough to marry me.

Waited for a honeymoon.

Waited for him to say something when things fell apart. I needed him to say something. I talked. And he seemed to listen, but when I asked how he felt, what he was thinking, he said nothing.

We went to couples therapy, and he still said nothing.

When I'd planned a getaway for us, he'd finally said something . . . no.

He didn't have time. He couldn't make time.

After I left, he'd finally said he wanted to talk, but to be honest, I'd done enough talking to last me a lifetime.

Then I waited again for him to realize there was no fixing us. I waited for him to file for our inevitable divorce.

But he didn't. He seemed content with the status quo.

Finally, I got as tired of waiting as I was of talking. Neither solved anything.

I took that last step myself. I thought I'd be done waiting.

Oh, the irony.

Here I was, waiting again. This time the waiting was worse than all the other times.

"I know, the waiting is the worst," James said.

I realized I must have said the word out loud and right after that I realized that James had come back. "Is Anne okay?"

"Fine. She's in recovery. They'll come get me when I can go back."

I nodded. "So you're waiting again."

"It's easier with someone waiting with you." He sat down, not in the seat he'd vacated, but next to me. "After I'm gone, you really should let your friend come down," he said again.

I nodded. "She'll be here when I need her. It doesn't matter what I say, she's the kind of friend who hears what I don't say just as clearly as what I do say."

He nodded. "It's good to have a friend like that."

It was. I patted James' hand, just as Maude had patted mine.

I didn't consider myself a big toucher. I found social hugs awkward. I never knew when one was appropriate and was always caught off guard when someone hugged me.

But here I was, patting James' hand, just as Maude had patted mine. I didn't feel awkward in the least.

Maybe it was a comrade-in-arms sort of thing. We were all here under fire. Maude had waited for her Bertie. James for his Anne. And me for Gray.

Talking to them had forced me to move past that one bitter moment in my relationship with Gray and start to remember other memories . . . the happier ones.

"Maybe sometimes we don't need a friend who knows our stories," I said. "Maybe sometimes we need someone new who doesn't know them. Someone who makes us look into the past. I know that doesn't sound like it makes sense, but I'd forgotten how happy Gray and I were that night as we drank cheap wine and talked about the future. Thank you for reminding me."

I had a mental image of Gray on an operating table, his ribs cracked open. I could see it so clearly. I'm sure I'd seen something like that on some medical show. I could hear the sound of a saw and hear the bones breaking—

James squeezed my hand as if he could sense what I was thinking. "So tell me about another moment you and your husband were that happy."

It struck me as absurd that for the last year I'd concentrated on the moments that had made me unhappy—the moments that had wounded me to the core.

Maybe I'd forgotten just how many happier moments there were.

"Gray and I talked about getting married from that night on. He said as soon as his business was standing on its own two feet we'd make it official. I'd reconciled myself to the idea of waiting years. I knew that most new businesses didn't survive, and those that did took years to become stable. I knew the company was doing all right, but Gray caught me totally off guard when he finally asked. I'd found a place for myself at Harbor House. I loved working with the clients and helping translate their vision into reality.

"You might think that a chair is just a chair, but when it's done right, it can be a work of art. Functional, useful, but ultimately, art. And Gray and Ash were working so hard to get Steel, Inc. off the ground. But one afternoon Gray called and asked me to have dinner with him . . .

ꟼ ꟼ ꟼ

I waited for Gray in front of my apartment.

"Wear something comfortable," he'd said when he'd called an hour earlier.

Normally those words at this time of year meant a picnic on the beach.

Gray took me often, though he said he didn't understand my penchant for watching a sunset. After all, the sun set every day, and he felt if you'd seen one sunset, you'd seen them all. I tried to explain that every sunset was different. Sometimes it was a subtle difference; sometimes it was a huge one. It didn't matter—each change could alter the entire experience. And even if they were all exactly the same, each time we came, we were altered—even if only by being a day older. And viewing things through a different lens changed everything.

As much as he complained, I suspected he enjoyed them as much as I did. During the summer he made an effort to bring me out to the peninsula often.

I'd gone to the state of Washington with my parents when I was twelve. We'd all watched a sunset on a rocky beach there. Afterward we all agreed that Lake Erie sunsets were just as beautiful . . . and possibly more so.

At the ocean there's a smell of salt in the air. There's a different thrum to the sound of the waves. Almost deeper. As if the weight of that whole ocean reverberated through each wave as it crashed onto the shore.

The vista on the lake—my lake—was as expansive as an ocean view, but the waves sounded smaller, more manageable. The large stone breakwalls at Presque Isle were covered with seagulls, and their cries frequently harmonized with the beat of the waves. And the smell was something else entirely. There, underneath the slightly fishy aroma that punctuates every large body of water, was a sweetness. A hint of pine and poplar trees.

As I waited for Gray, I wondered about the differences between ocean and lake sunsets, knowing that I would always prefer my lake.

Gray pulled up in front of my old college apartment. I'd thought about moving into something bigger, something more adult, after I'd graduated, but I'd gotten comfortable here. I didn't need much space.

I got in his car and saw a picnic basket on the backseat.

"I was right," I said as I climbed into the passenger seat. I leaned over and kissed his cheek. "You know I love sunset picnics."

He shook his head. "Not tonight, though we can make it a point of going out next week."

There was a flash of happiness in his eyes. "This is something new," he said. "A surprise."

Wherever we were going might be new, but this teasing, surprising side of Gray was newer still. Graham Grayson was not a man given to unexpected things, nor was he a man who was prone to teasing.

"Give me a hint?" I wheedled.

He shook his head. "Be patient."

"I think that maybe I missed the patience line when they were handing out virtues," I told him, not for the first time. "To be honest, I think we both know that there's no maybe *about it."*

"I might not have gotten a full dose either," he said.

I snorted at his statement, then laughed when I realized that he actually believed what he'd said. "You are the most patient, methodical man I've ever met. You set a goal and then work your way toward it, one step after the next. You never seem to get sidetracked or frustrated. You just keep moving toward that goal with utter assurance you'll reach it."

"I am not as patient as you think," he said cryptically. I noticed he drove with his hands at ten and two, just like the drivers' manuals said. There was a slight paleness to his knuckles, as if he was clenching the steering wheel harder than necessary.

I stopped teasing and asked, "Gray, are you all right?"

He nodded. "I'm fine, of course. I'm with you, aren't I?"

Gray was not a man who waxed poetic. To be honest, he didn't wax much of anything. Most of the time I did the talking for both of us. So, his I'm-with-you-aren't-I was probably one of the most romantic things he ever said.

As I swooned over it, he added, "But, for the record, sometimes I set a goal and realize it's unrealistic, then I rethink things. I am capable of changing directions."

I snorted again. I'd yet to find an instance where Gray altered his course. But I was too happy to argue the point.

"So where are we going?" I asked, thinking my question might catch him unaware.

I should have known better.

"We'll be there soon," he answered.

"Captain Cryptic strikes again," I muttered.

Gray reached State Street and headed south. State Street started at the bay and split the city into an east and a west side. It also split the city's downtown park, Perry Square, in half.

I loved driving through Perry Square. They'd spent the last few years sprucing it up and I thought it looked lovely with its welcoming arches and its fountain.

Beyond Perry Square we passed City Hall, which sat on the west side of the street, and a couple of blocks up from the historic Warner Theater, which sat on the east side.

I found myself counting the streets, whose number increased as Gray drove away from the bay. Twelfth Street, Thirteenth . . .

We reached Thirty-Eighth Street and I was sure he'd take this other main street either east or west. Once he picked a direction, I might have a chance at guessing our destination.

But he kept driving. At Forty-First, he turned right, then a couple of blocks later, turned left, so we were heading south again, on Willow Lane.

He pulled the car over to the side of the road and said, "Let's go."

"Where are we?" I might have thought we were going to some colleague's house, but if so he'd have asked me to dress up, not down.

"You'll see," he said.

"Mr. Mysterious allies with his pal Captain Cryptic on another mad adventure," I said in my best radio-broadcaster voice. "Join them in tonight's episode as they set out with their sidekicks, Obie Obscure and Peter Perplexing—"

Gray interrupted, uncharacteristically joining in my weirdness. He did a mean radio-broadcaster voice as well. "As they set out to woo Addled Adeline—"

"Hey," I protested. I muttered as I got out of the car, "The 'addled' part wasn't nice, but I did like the wooing part."

"I hope you like the rest of the surprise," he said.

Gray grabbed the picnic basket. It was his mom's, so there was a good chance Peggy had helped him pack our dinner.

His mom was an amazing cook. I frequently teased her that she should consider cooking instead of waitressing, but she laughed and told me that cooks get no tips so she'd be wasting her innumerable charms.

Gray walked to a gate in front of an unfamiliar house. It squeaked softly as he pushed it open. There was a wrought-iron fence that reached my waist. The gate, however, was taller. It was the same as the rest of the fence, but the top extended into a circle, beyond which I could see a well-manicured lawn that was split by a brick sidewalk.

That sidewalk led to a small, L-shaped, brick home that had a touch of a Tudor element.

Ivy draped around the arched front door.

This was a home that could be part of a fairy tale. I could imagine some princess in disguise waiting here for her prince.

"It's adorable. Whose is it?" I asked.

"That's the surprise," he said, no less cryptic than he'd been in the car.

The grass-covered lawn was meticulously trimmed, as were the boxwood hedges that lined the porch.

We reached the arched doorway and Gray set down the basket, reached out, and opened the door. "Gray, you can't—"

He cut off my protest as he scooped me up and carried me into what I quickly saw was an empty house.

"Do you like it?" he asked as he set me down on a wide-planked, hardwood floor that had some wear. But rather than make it look neglected, the slight imperfections made it look homey. Inviting.

There was a bank of three windows, three-by-threes, and across from the windows was a brick fireplace that was flanked by built-in shelves.

"It's beautiful," I assured him.

There it was again . . . that smile I so loved. "It's yours if you want it," he said.

"Pardon?"

"I know you love Glenwood Hills and Tudor-style homes. When Ash and I were looking for an office, I mentioned to the agent that if he ever saw a screaming deal on something like this in Glenwood, he should call me. He remembered and called yesterday."

The real estate agent called yesterday and we were here today? That sort of timeline was so not Gray-like at all. "And you bought it?"

"He's got the paperwork on his desk right now. I just needed to know that you liked it before I had him make the offer."

"This is your house, so it shouldn't matter if I like it." It shouldn't matter, but I knew the moment I said the words, it would. Gray was asking if one day, when we married, I could live here.

"No, it would be our house," he said.

I smiled, realizing how well I knew this man I loved.

Then he reached in his pocket and pulled out a ring box. "If you still say yes."

And at that moment, I realized that even if I knew him, he could still surprise me. I—who normally had enough words to fill in both sides of our conversations—was suddenly speechless.

"Gray" was all I could manage.

Graham Grayson was a man who planned everything out to the minutest detail. But this? The agent had called yesterday. And here we were this evening. And there he was with a ring.

My world had tilted.

"Addie, I need you to say the word," he prompted.

I took the ring box from him. "Yes. Of course, it's yes. It will always be yes. Yes."

He smiled then. And it occurred to me that despite my previous assurance, he'd been nervous.

"And the house?" he asked.

I looked at the empty living room and nodded. "If you think we can afford it, yes as well."

I thought he'd kiss me then, but instead, he pulled his phone out of his pocket and dialed. "Make the offer," he said.

I opened the ring box and pulled the small diamond ring out of it.

"I'd planned something more elaborate, but if we're buying the house, I can't afford anything more right now. But someday I'll replace it with something bigger," he promised.

"Don't you dare. This is perfect." I slipped it on my ring finger and it fit perfectly. I'm not sure how Gray had gotten my size, but as always, he was meticulous. "The ring and even the house aren't what I'll remember about today," I told him. "I'll remember that you asked and I said yes."

"I was nervous," he admitted. "It's not the way I planned it."

"You and your plans," I teasingly scolded. "Life happens while you're making plans. I think I realized that first day of school when you took me under your wing that I was part of you. And you were and are most assuredly part of me. I definitely knew that my world was better when I had you in it."

And then, the waiting was over. He finally kissed me. "I love you."

Those three words sealed the deal. The house, the ring . . . none of it mattered as much as those three words.

I touched my thumb to the ring that bound us together in the living room of a house he'd bought us. A house where we'd live and raise a famiyl . . .

ꟻ ꟻ ꟻ

I pulled myself back from the memory, my thumb still touching the ring I still wore. "The agent called before we finished our picnic. The sellers had accepted Gray's offer," I told James.

"And so did you," James said.

I nodded. "Even without the house, I'd have accepted. I didn't need fanfare, I just needed him and three little words."

James quirked his eyebrow and I knew the question, just as I thought he already knew the answer.

"*I love you.* Just those three words."

He nodded, understanding.

I clutched the envelope. I was very aware of the rings that I still wore on my ring finger.

Why hadn't I taken them off when I'd decided to divorce him?

Force of habit?

Or was it something more?

I felt a resurgence of those old feelings. It was as if the warmth of that long-ago day had somehow been rekindled.

"I know you said he was a planner, but that all sounded very spontaneous," James said.

"It was. He caught me unaware." I had thought I knew Gray inside and out. I liked that there was a constancy about him. I knew I could count on him . . . always. And I'd known when I took him the divorce papers I could count on his reaction. He'd see the logic and we'd part as . . .

Well, maybe not friends, but we'd part friendly. If I called him, I knew no matter how many years stood between us, he'd come. And vice versa.

"Maybe your husband simply couldn't stick to his timetable. Maybe he couldn't wait another minute to marry you."

I shrugged. It would be nice to think so, but I thought it was more likely that Gray had decided the deal on the house made passing it up out of the question. And he'd probably budgeted for both our incomes in order to afford it.

I hadn't thought of that at the time, but it had occurred to me since.

James continued, "Sometimes it's hard to wait for what you want . . . sometimes it's impossible. I know that waiting for Anne to get better has become impossible for our friends. But I'll wait as long as it takes."

His voice dropped to almost a whisper. "She worries that she will never get back to her old self. That she'll be less than who she was. I keep telling her less of her means more to me than any other person in this world. I'll wait as long as it takes for a chance at just one more day with her."

As I looked at James, so willing to wait for his Anne—willing to have her back in any state—I envied his patience.

And I wondered if maybe I gave up too easily?

If I should have waited a little longer?

Chapter Five

I sat with James for another half hour until the nurse came and got him. "Mr. Patterson, your wife is awake and asking for you."

I squeezed his hand before he got up. "Good luck. I hope that Anne's recovery is quick."

"Me, too," he said. "Good luck to your husband. I hope you don't have to wait much longer."

I watched as he walked out of the room next to the nurse. There was more of a lift in his shoulders, as if he was lighter now that the weight of his waiting had ended.

I missed him when he left.

It was odd to feel a connection to someone you'd just met—someone you knew so very little about.

I knew his name was James with an S and he was married to Anne with an E. And I knew that he loved her.

Maybe all the rest didn't mean so much after all. Maybe what mattered was a man named James loved a woman named Anne and planned to wait as long as it took to have more time with her.

I'd always thought my love for Gray was limitless, but looking back, it couldn't have been. I placed a limit on it. The evidence of that was in my hand.

I'd proven that I wasn't willing to wait any longer.

And I wondered if that was because of Gray . . . or because of some inherent flaw in me.

No one sat in James' seat. And I was left alone with only the hum of the televisions and bits of conversations as my companions.

Images from old television shows collided with my fears for Gray. People calling codes. Crash carts. Doctors in scrubs throwing bloody pads on the floor.

I desperately wished James or Maude would come back and distract me from my imagination.

And as if on cue, JoAnn appeared and sat in James' vacant seat, just as I'd assured him she would.

"I brought you granola and a charger," she said by way of a greeting and handed me a baggie filled with dried fruit and nuts and a charger. "And coffee. And this . . ."

She leaned over and hugged me. "Harmon said he'll check in with you, and Wills said to be sure I told you he peed in the potty. If you want to be accurate, he peed pretty much everywhere but the potty, but it was the attempt that mattered. You know what they say about being perfect in the attempt. Don't tell him, but I'll be even happier when he's perfect with his aim, too. And before you ask, I'll assure you that yes, I potty danced for the victory."

As she said the words, she did a little wiggle in her chair. A ghost of a potty dance. Despite the heaviness of waiting, I couldn't help but laugh.

I knew that had been JoAnn's intent.

"Whoever knew that one day my children's bathroom antics would be such a frequent topic of my conversations?" she asked.

I smiled. "You love every minute of it."

"Wrong. I don't enjoy cleaning up after Wills attempts peeing standing up. But otherwise, yes." She patted my hand. "Bathroom exploits aside, I called Tom into work. I don't want you to worry about a thing. I've got everything managed. Everyone at the store is pitching in, and they all send their love. I've got to get back soon."

"Oh, Jo, I'm sorry. What about the kids?" She didn't leave them more than for an hour or so with her neighbor. She still worked part-time, but only during hours when Harmon would be home with the kids. She often said she couldn't wait until they were both safely tucked up in school so she could return to work full time, but I think we both knew that when that day came, she'd be heartbroken.

"Listen, the kids are fine without me for a few days. To be honest, they're probably sick of me and welcome the change of venue." She laughed as if it were a joke. I knew she wanted me to laugh as well. She was trying to lighten my mood, if only for a moment. But I couldn't manage it.

She nodded as if she understood. "Joey's taking a nap. Leslie's going to drop him off with me at the store when he wakes up, but she'll keep Wills."

"JoAnn—"

"Listen, you remember when I used to come into the store with Wills when he was an infant. The sales went through the roof. I am going to blatantly use Joey as my sales ace in the hole, too. I just dropped in to bring you something to eat and give you a hug and share a new, scintillating story of my adventures in potty training. Everything's fine with the store. The entire staff is picking up hours for you. I've got the next week scheduled. We'll play it by ear after that."

"I don't need a week—" I started to protest.

JoAnn shook her head. "Honey, I know you. You're not leaving until Gray leaves here. And if they're doing surgery, he'll be here for a while. Is there anything else you need? Your iPad? Your iPod?"

"I don't need anything. Really. And I lost my iPod when I moved out and haven't bothered getting a new one."

That was an utterly random piece of information and I had no idea why I said it. I just shrugged.

She nodded as if that information was of the utmost importance to her. "For the next week, don't worry about the store or anything else. I've got it. You just worry about yourself and Gray. And remember, all of us are here for you. You call and I'll come running."

"Even if I don't call, you'll come running," I said with certainty.

A tear fell. It landed on my hand, then rolled onto the divorce papers, creating a new little smudge next to the coffee one.

"I didn't tell him," I said in a whisper.

"I didn't tell him," I said again, a little louder this time.

"Tell who what? Gray?" JoAnn asked.

"I didn't give Gray the papers. I didn't tell him I was divorcing him. He was talking about ice cream and waiting for me, and I thought maybe . . . But I think he knew why I was there, though. What if my going to his office suddenly made it real? What if that's why he had a heart attack?"

Maybe his being here was my fault. It felt as if the universe was being perverse. After all, I'd said I was done with Gray. And now, I might be, on a permanent basis.

For months, I'd been stuck at our worst moment. I couldn't see what had come before it. Now, thanks to Maude and James, I was remembering the other moments—the better moments—and I wasn't sure if I'd survive losing him.

I'd thought I'd missed him in the vast silence before I left, but now—knowing I could lose him permanently—I realized that void was nothing compared to what I'd face if he died.

"It wasn't a heart attack, remember?" JoAnn said gently. "I looked up an aortic dissection after you called. It was something he'd had for a while. There can be a genetic component. Mainly they happen with people much older than us, so that would be my guess, not that I'm a doctor."

"You don't know that." I didn't know, so she couldn't know. "What if my being there exacerbated the situation?" I asked, voicing my secret fear.

I rubbed the spot where my tear had fallen on the envelope. It left a mark.

"Then you saved his life," she said with surety. "What if he'd been home alone when it happened? You wouldn't have been there to call for help. You didn't do this to him, Addie."

Even in the fog I was trying to think through, I realized logically JoAnn was right. Just as quickly I realized that being *right* didn't matter.

Logic and feelings had nothing whatsoever to do with each other. And I felt as if it were my fault.

I also realized that I hadn't set the divorce papers down because I felt as if I had to hold on to them.

I wasn't sure if they had become my talisman or a scarlet letter.

"Addie, are you sure you're okay? I can stay," JoAnn offered.

She would. She'd juggle and restructure her plans to be with me. "No. I'll feel better if I know you're at the store."

"You know that you mean more to me than the store, right?" she asked. "I love you, Addie."

"More than pickles?" I asked. That was her phrase for Wills and Joey. *I love you more than . . .* She always started out with pickles, and then added to her list. Pickles. Pizza. Ice cream.

"I most definitely love you more than pickles," she assured me.

I'd commented once that most of her *more thans* were food. Afterward she'd made an effort to include nonfood items.

Which was probably why she added, "And I love you more than sunsets."

I reached over and took her hand. "Ditto" was all I said because that was all that needed to be said.

Hands weren't enough . . . she hugged me again. "You are my best friend, Adeline. I'll be here whenever you need me for as long as you need me."

"I knew that before you walked in. But right now, I really need to be alone. I have to think and sort things out." I felt another tear gather in the corner of my eye, but I blinked it back. I knew she'd never leave if she thought I needed her.

She studied me a moment, then nodded again. "I'm a phone call away. And I'll be back later."

"Thank you."

"You can thank me by eating something." She leaned down and kissed my cheek as if I were one of her boys. "More than pickles," she whispered.

"Or sunsets," I responded.

I watched as JoAnn left.

I lost my parents before I graduated from college and had no extended relatives I was close to. But I'd never lacked for family.

I read a book when I was in grade school about a couple who'd adopted all their children. Their family was made, not born. Their family was bound by love, not by blood.

That's how it was with JoAnn. She was my family . . . not by blood, but by love.

I loved her more than sunsets.

Or pickles.

And I knew she'd be there for me, whenever I called.

There was a comfort in that.

Chapter Six

JoAnn had been gone for more than an hour.

I didn't cry anymore, mainly because I had a feeling that if I started to cry again, there was a chance I wouldn't be able to stop.

I'd managed to nibble at the granola JoAnn had brought me, not because I had an appetite, but so I could tell her I'd eaten.

I kept catching myself staring at the woman sitting across from me, her nose buried in a book. I forced myself to look at the television screen, but I couldn't follow what was going on. I wished I could read the way she did.

Anything to take me away from here and now. Television was obviously not going to do it.

I opened my *Kindle* app on my phone. Reading on my phone wasn't my favorite way to read, but it would do in a pinch. I loved that I always had a book with me. Whenever we had to wait for something, I'd open up my current read and be content.

It amused Gray. He rarely said anything, but he'd roll his eyes and that little ghost of a smile would play across his lips whenever I opened the app.

I closed my eyes and could almost see that smile.

And I caught myself wondering if I'd ever see it again.

I pushed the thought aside, opened my eyes, and tried to read, but I don't think I'd managed a whole page before I realized that for the first time in my life a book couldn't take me away from the real world.

I glanced at the reader across from me again and felt a stab of jealousy that she could.

The woman who'd taken James' seat looked up from her book, as if she could either feel my eyes upon her, or sense my book-envy.

"Have you read it?" she asked kindly as she held the book up.

I shook my head. "No. I was wishing I could escape into a book. I've always been able to manage it, but I can't today." I flashed her my phone screen. I wasn't even sure I could tell her what book I'd opened.

She nodded. "To be honest, I think I've read the same page five or six times. It seemed easier to pretend to read than to sit here staring into space." She must have realized that staring into space summed up what I'd been doing because she said, "Sorry."

"No, you're right. That's exactly what I've been doing."

"Who are you waiting for?" she asked.

How to describe my relationship with Gray? I went for the most accepted definition, "my husband," but given the papers in my hand, I wasn't sure that was true. "You?"

"My daughter." There was a catch in her voice as she said the word *daughter*.

"I'm so sorry." Having Gray here was awful, but to be a mother and have to sit by while your child was sick? Once I might not have completely understood how awful that would be, but now I did.

"Thank you," she whispered. "She's only fourteen. She woke up in horrible pain. They said it was her appendix. As a mother, I can remind her to eat right and wear her seatbelt. I can make sure she gets enough rest and studies for tests. But I can't protect her from her own body. And I know it's stupid, but I feel like I should be able to."

I understood her need to protect her daughter. "I think that need to protect your children is embedded in our DNA."

"Do you have children?" she asked.

I shook my head and found myself answering her honestly. More honestly than a stranger deserved. "I've always wanted them. My husband wanted us to wait. He wanted to have everything in place financially before we had kids. We hardly ever fought, but we did about this one issue. If he hadn't wanted kids, I might have been able to understand. But he did . . ."

I didn't go any further with my answer because the rest was too hard.

The book reader didn't seem to notice. "Ruby was a change-of-life baby. I was in my forties and thought I was just going through an abnormally early menopause." She chuckled at the memory. "I spent two weeks crying once I figured out I was pregnant. But after that . . ." She shrugged. "The pregnancy was so easy that I forgot about her for long periods of time. Life just sort of went on as it always had. Then she was born and was the easiest baby in the history of babies."

My mother had always said I was an easygoing baby. Peggy had said repeatedly that Gray was not. He was high needs and she swore he had some sort of allergy to sleep. He'd never needed more than four or five hours a day. He still didn't . . . unless things had changed since I left.

All those months of not talking.

What if he'd found out he had some heart issue during that time? Would he have told me?

I didn't think so.

Gray wasn't a man who was prone to sharing his worries and burdens in the best of circumstances. And he and I weren't anywhere close to being in a best of circumstances. Not for us. Not for our marriage.

I clenched the envelope in my hand.

I could shove it in my purse. Out of sight, out of mind. But I knew I wouldn't. I needed it as a reminder. I'd given up on Gray. Fair or not, I felt he'd failed me and I'd stopped trying.

Gray had always needed me to try. He was someone prone to isolation.

In another lifetime I could see him finding a contented life in some remote monastery. Not speaking. I could see him achieving his monkly objectives with the same fierce intensity that he used for Steel, Inc.

I didn't ask this woman's name. I didn't ask her any more about her daughter. Maybe that made me selfish, but I wasn't sure I could handle suffering for one more person. Maude, Bertie, James, Anne *with an E*, and now this woman's daughter, Ruby, were all the worries I could handle on top of my own. I didn't want to know her name.

I was trying to decide how to pull back from the conversation without seeming rude, when someone behind me called, "Harriet Mumford?"

The book reader was Harriet Mumford.

Now I knew, even if I didn't want to. I was right. Knowing her name made her seem even more real, which made her pain and her worry more tangible as well.

Harriet bounded from her chair as if on a spring, tossing her book on the seat next to her coat and purse. I turned and watched her talking to the nurse or doctor. They all had on scrubs and I couldn't tell one from another.

Harriet smiled.

I let out a breath I hadn't known I was holding.

Her daughter was okay. I wish I knew if Bertie and Anne were.

But selfishly, more than that I wished the doctor would come down and tell me about Gray.

Harriet Mumford came back to her seat, practically radiating happiness. She picked up her coat, purse, and the book. "I'm going to meet with the doctor, but the nurse said Ruby's going to be fine," she said.

I took her hand. "I'm so happy for you."

"Thank you."

Before I could say anything else, she was already gone, anxious to see her daughter.

Moments before I'd wanted to withdraw from our conversation, but now that Harriet Mumford was gone, the waiting room felt lonely.

I stared blankly at the television, ignoring the conversations around me. The memories I'd shared with Maude and James seemed to have opened a floodgate. Moments from my life with Gray kept worming their way into the forefront of my mind.

A commercial that touted the best dishwashing soap ever made me remember a night when Gray had offered to help me with the dishes.

"You wash, I'll dry," he offered.

I ran the water and added a generous squirt of dish soap. The sink was soon full of suds and dirty dishes.

I handed Gray the first cup and he dried it with meticulous thoroughness before setting it down and reaching for the next cup from the rack.

I kept glancing at him as we worked in companionable silence. He looked so serious as he worked. I wanted to see him smile—not just wanted, needed—so I scooped up a handful of bubbles and blew them in Gray's face.

He didn't react. Instead, he finished drying the cup in his hand and then casually took his towel and wiped the bubbles off his nose. I thought our impromptu bubble-battle was over, but he surprised me.

He reached into the sink, grabbed a handful of bubbles, and, rather than blowing them at me, he smooshed them into my face.

"Hey," I hollered. I grabbed another handful, ready to retaliate, but Gray was ready for me. He grabbed my wrist and pushed it into my hair.

Still holding on to my wrist, he pulled me into his arms and kissed me. The kiss tasted of soap and love . . . so much love.

He scooped me up and carried me upstairs.

The dishes didn't get washed until the next morning.

How had I forgotten moments like that?

Everyone I spoke to reminded me of something.

Everything I saw on the television did as well.

A kid throwing spitwads in class on television reminded me of an afternoon—I had no idea how long ago it was, though it felt like a lifetime ago. Gray had been working on some figures for the business and I'd been filling out some forms for Harbor House. I'd made a football out of a piece of paper. The same kind we'd made in grade school. I'd flicked it expertly at Gray. It had landed in the center of his paper.

He didn't say a word, but he looked up and his serious, business expression melted into a smile. Then he'd picked up the paper football and flicked it back at me, with just as much expert aim.

We both went back to our respective work, but for the next few hours, the paper football periodically volleyed back and forth.

When he finished working he'd simply said, "Love you."

I still had the football in my jewelry box, next to my plastic drink swan. It was a strange memento, but it had been such a lovely afternoon. The two of us working independently, but together.

I could almost hear him. "Love you."

I think those small moments were the ones that kept creeping into my thoughts because they were the ones I missed the most.

I didn't look back longingly at major events. Not our wedding. Not the big Steel, Inc. gala parties. Not the big moments for Harbor House.

I missed paper footballs and washing dishes together . . . or not washing dishes together, as the case may be.

I missed Gray.

I missed him so much I almost ached with it.

How had I not noticed how much I missed him?

Then I remembered.

I'd missed him long before I'd walked out of our house on February third. To be honest, I think he left me on December second. The months before that, I'd never felt closer to him, but that day we'd lost everything, I lost him . . .

"Mrs. Grayson?" Another woman wearing scrubs stood in the doorway to the waiting room. The difference was, this time she was calling my name.

Part of me wanted to bound out of my seat like Harriet the book reader had. But a bigger part of me was terrified and seemed to be rooted to the spot.

If I didn't go see this woman, Gray was still in surgery. His fate was still in limbo.

And limbo was so much better than bad news.

"Mrs. Grayson," she called again, this time with a tinge of frustration in her voice.

I looked in her direction and knew I had to get up and go get the news, but still I hesitated. Finally she came to me.

"Mrs. Grayson?" she asked.

I nodded.

"If you'll follow me, I'll get you set up in the consult room. The doctor is on her way down."

I nodded and got up to follow her.

I was relieved Gray's fate was still in limbo.

I was terrified that all too soon I'd know.

The small room the nurse escorted me to had two chairs, a small table, and two doors. I entered through one door and the nurse closed it behind me.

I knew that I was expected to sit in one of the chairs, but despite the fact my knees felt weak, I couldn't seem to.

The room was private. Probably because it was easier if they had to deliver bad news.

Easier on the doctors because they could get up and leave through their back door.

Easier on the other families who were waiting to hear the outcome of their loved ones.

I paced back and forth. The room was six steps from wall to wall.

I wasn't claustrophobic, but this small, windowless room was oppressive. I stood in the center, closed my eyes, and tried to picture my view of Presque Isle from the Ferncliff house, but instead I saw my room on Willow Lane.

I was in bed, propped against a pillow, watching Gray in the bathroom shaving.

The sheets were freshly laundered. I'd hung them outside and they smelled of summer air.

I could almost smell the shaving cream as I watched him tilt his head this way and that, scraping the stubble from his face. He leaned over and splashed water on his cheeks and as he reached for the towel, he spotted me watching him.

His expression changed. He didn't smile, but rather he looked at me. And in his gaze, I could see desire, but more than that, I could see love.

I reached for him, and without words, he understood my need . . .

I wished I could reach for him now.

I opened my eyes and again felt as if the walls were closing in.

Where was the doctor?

Would she tell me he was going to be fine or . . .

No, there was no *or*. He would be fine. Gray was the strongest man I'd ever known. He had more determination than any man I'd ever met. He wouldn't leave me.

He couldn't leave me. We had ice cream in the freezer at Willow Lane waiting for us, so he couldn't go yet.

And then I remembered that in a way, he'd left me months ago.

But a small, honest voice reminded me I'd been the one to leave the house.

The doctor came in with a grim expression and a tablet. I clutched my manila envelope as if it were a lifeline. Maybe it was, in a way. When I'd brought the papers to Gray, he'd been alive and healthy; his name was on them, marking his permanence.

The doctor didn't seem to care that I hadn't sat down. She took a seat and as if in slow motion tapped something on her tablet and then as if remembering me, said, "Mrs. Grayson. The surgery progressed as expected."

I thought she'd been going to tell me he was gone.

I let out a breath I hadn't realized I was holding. My knees felt wobbly so I finally sank into the other chair. "So he's going to be okay?"

She shook her head. "He's still touch and go. He's in recovery now, but he'll be heading to ICU so we can monitor him."

"But I can see him?"

She nodded. "But you need to be prepared. We're keeping him in a medically induced coma. The medication we're using means that he needs help breathing. So he'll be hooked up to a ventilator to help him breathe. He has IVs; there are monitors. He's not going to know you're there."

Coma. Not a coma like he'd been in an accident and might not wake up, but one that the doctors were using to keep him asleep. "How long?"

"Mrs. Grayson, we need to get your husband's blood pressure under control. We'll keep him sedated until we do. It could be hours or days. Days are more likely."

"And if you can't get his blood pressure under control?" I asked.

"The stent we just put in won't be able to do its job. The results would be catastrophic."

I understood what she was saying by using the word *catastrophic*. If he blew out that stent, I would lose him. I nodded. "I can see him?"

"Yes. But the visiting hours are strict in ICU. They need an hour to get him settled in the unit, then you may see him. The nurses will fill you in on the specifics, but they generally want to give the patient a quiet night. So they'll be sending you home when visiting hours are over."

"I planned on staying with him," I admitted.

"Most families say that, but it's better for the patient if they get a quiet night, and frankly, ma'am, it's better for the families." There was a kindness in her voice now, not just a brisk recitation of facts. "When a patient is in the ICU it generally means that their hospital stay isn't going to be a sprint, but a marathon. When we finally wake your husband up, he'll need physical therapy. He'll need to make some lifestyle changes. You need to take care of yourself in order to take care of him when he is released."

She stood as if she'd decided she'd given me all the information I needed.

Gray had made it through surgery, but he was still touch and go.

Gray would be in ICU. He'd be in a medically induced coma. He'd have tubes and wires galore. He wouldn't know me.

His condition wouldn't be a sprint, but rather a marathon.

"The nurses will fill you in with any updates when you go upstairs," she said.

I didn't get up as well, but just nodded.

She finally looked at me as if I were a person, not some obligation she had to meet. "Why don't you go get something to eat?" she asked gently. "When you're done, you should be able to go up to the fourth floor and see him."

"Thank you." I still sat in the chair.

She reached out and squeezed my shoulder. "I had the easy part. You're going to have the hard part. When he wakes up you're going to have to convince him to make some changes."

Changing Gray wasn't simply difficult; it was impossible.

I went out the patient door as the doctor went out the one she'd entered. Book reader—Harriet Mumford—was back in her chair.

"Is he okay?" she asked.

I nodded. "So far so good. I can go up and see him in an hour. The doctor is sending me to get something to eat."

She shut the book and stood. "They said I can't see Ruby for at least that long. Why don't I come with you? I'll let the nurse here know where I am and she'll get me if she needs me."

We checked in with the nurse who sat at a desk in the back of the waiting room. "I'll definitely come get you if anything happens. Getting something to eat is a great idea," she said with more pep than was probably necessary. "Just turn left and walk until you find the plant, then turn left again."

"You use the plant as a landmark?" I asked.

The nurse smiled. "It's artificial, and because we're in a windowless section of the hospital, it does stand out."

We made our way down to the cafeteria. It was on the same floor . . . the lowest floor of the hospital. There were windows in the dining room, however. They pressed against the ceiling and ran the length of the room. I couldn't see out of them, but I felt better seeing some natural light.

Harriet and I both got a salad. She got a bottle of water; I got some ice tea. Then we both played at pushing around our food.

"I just realized that I've eaten more than a couple of bites of my salad and forgot to put dressing on it," I said.

Harriet managed a small smile. "To be honest, I could be eating grass for as much as I'm tasting this. I know they said my daughter's fine, but I won't really *know* it until I see Ruby . . . until I hold her. I felt the same way when she was born. They said I had a daughter, but she didn't feel real until I held her. I don't think I've ever fallen so instantly in love with anyone or anything. The moment they told me I was pregnant, I was in love. Well, once I adjusted to the idea I had a baby, not menopause." She stopped. "Are you okay?"

I nodded, but it was a lie.

Her words took me back to a happy night. I couldn't decide if I'd tried to block the memory before, or if remembering that one happy moment had been simply too painful. But now, when the memory resurfaced, I didn't turn away from it. I embraced it.

ꟼ ꟼ ꟼ

I was sitting in our upstairs bathroom on the edge of the claw-foot bathtub.

I stared at the stick in my hand. The news didn't come as a surprise, but the confirmation made my suspicions real. I put my hand over my still-flat stomach. How would it feel as it expanded?

How would it feel to have a baby inside me, kicking?

How could I possibly wait all the months ahead of me to meet this baby who was part of me and part of Gray?

"I love you," I whispered, trying on the words for size. I didn't need a book on babies to know that mine was tiny and not fully formed yet. And yet, those three words were such a basic truth. I loved this baby. Love for this little boy or girl permeated every piece of my being and I knew that I'd never be the same now that I knew.

It was as if this moment marked a definite line in my life. Everything from here on out would either fall before-the-baby or after-the-baby.

"I love you," I whispered again. I would tell this baby every day of its life that I loved it.

Boy. Girl. It didn't matter. I was head over heels in love.

What a wonderful life this child would have.

I sat on the side of the bathtub and no longer saw the gray tiles or the large antique mirror I'd bought at an auction last year. All I could see were so many possible futures for the baby. Sports? Academics?

A reader? Would this baby be a reader and hide away, able to lose him or herself in the pages of a book like me?

I was already thinking about books I'd read to Wills and loved. I'd need copies for—

"Addie?"

I jumped from the side of the tub and landed on the cold tile.

Gray would love this child. I knew that. But he wanted to wait a while longer before we had kids. He had a timetable in his head and this was too soon. I knew that it might take him a little longer to adjust to the idea, just as I knew that once he did he'd be thrilled.

I took the little stick with me and hurried down the stairs.

"There you are," he said. "I thought maybe you got held up at work. I was going to call your cell."

He put his keys in the small bowl on the table to the left of the door . . . just as he always did.

He put his briefcase under the table . . . just as he always did.

Then he came to kiss me . . . just as he always did.

Gray was a man who thrived on routines and plans.

I wouldn't allow myself to be hurt if he took a moment to acclimate to our news, I warned myself.

"I left work early today," I said slowly, trying to find the perfect words to share our news.

Those were obviously not them, because he immediately looked concerned. "Are you okay?"

"Yes. I'm fine," I said. "It's just—"

"What's wrong?"

I was making a muck of this. I took a deep breath and tried to come at the news slowly. "Gray, do you remember back in college when you told me someday you'd ask me to marry you and I said whenever you asked, I'd say yes?"

He nodded slowly. "I don't know what's going on."

"Give me a second. Back then, you had our future all laid out in your head. You'd build a successful business, and when you were financially stable, you'd ask me to marry you."

"Yes," he said slowly.

"Then you found this house and asked me sooner than in that original plan."

He nodded again. "Sometimes plans have to shift and alter."

I grinned. "Yes, that's just it. Sometimes life happens and takes an unexpected turn. And that can be good. After all, it all worked out, didn't it? I mean, you're happy?"

He put his hands on my hips and pulled me closer. "Addie, of course I'm happy. I love you."

There they were . . . those three words.

"And I love you," I assured him.

"So what's going on?" he asked.

"I wanted to remind you that I understand you like to plan things out, but sometimes, life won't allow itself to be scheduled, and even if something happens that's not what you planned, that can be okay."

"What is going on?" he asked again.

I held out the stick.

"What is . . ." He didn't finish the question. I saw the dawning of understanding on his face.

"You're pregnant?" he asked softly. I nodded.

He stood still for a long moment. And slowly, his look of surprise gave way to happiness. Utter, complete happiness.

Maybe because his expressions were so frequently inscrutable, moments like this stood out more clearly. Because there was nothing mysterious in his expression of joy. He pulled me that last step into his arms and hugged me.

"I know this wasn't how you planned it," I said.

"To hell with my plans," he said. "We're going to have a baby."

I know that I'd been in pain, but how had I forgotten that moment and Gray's utter joy at the thought of having a child? I pressed my hands to my flat stomach and felt an ache. An ache that would never truly be healed. The memory was sweet and poignant and it made me wonder how I ever thought I could give him the papers in my other hand.

We had spent the rest of that night talking about our baby and dreaming about what sort of life he or she would have. I saw the memory in a rosy glow. It was a moment of true and utter happiness for both Gray and me.

I didn't share this particular memory with Harriet. I didn't talk about our son with anyone. Neither did Gray.

Maybe we should have. And not just talked to each other, but friends. I knew that JoAnn would have listened, but I didn't know what to say, so in the end, I said nothing.

Harriet and I both threw out our salads and walked back to the waiting room.

"Mrs. Grayson?" the nurse said. "You can go up now."

I nodded. "Thank you," I told Harriet. "I hope your daughter is okay."

"I hope the same for your husband."

We took each other's hand and squeezed it.

I might never see her again, but, like Maude and James, I would remember her. She'd given me back the gift of that memory. That one beautiful moment of utter contentment and joy.

As I walked out of the waiting room, that one memory helped me bear the weight of the waiting.

Chapter Seven

I left the operating waiting room and tried to retrace my path to the elevators. I took one wrong turn, then saw the signs for the elevator and followed them.

I passed two open doors I hadn't noticed before.

It was a chapel. I peeked in. There were a few rows of chairs, and at the front was more of a long table than an altar, behind which hung long drapes.

There were two people sitting in the room: a woman who was leaning against a man's shoulder. I wondered if they were family or friends, or, like Harriet, James, and Maude, were simply two people sharing a horrible moment together.

Delving into my memories had eased my anxiety, at least for a minute. I hoped that revisiting a Piggly Wiggly, or remembering Anne's E, or the joy of loving a child had softened the pain of Maude, James, and Harriet's waiting as well.

I continued down the hall to the bank of elevators and rode one to the fourth floor. I followed the signs down the hall. A nurse greeted me. "Can I help you?"

"I'm here to see . . . Graham Grayson." I hesitated over his name. Referring to him as Graham was difficult.

"This way, ma'am," a nurse with a harried look about her said as she ushered me toward what was more of an opening than a proper door.

Gray's room was little more than a cubby. It held a small window, a bed, a chair, and machines.

Gray had always seemed so solid and strong. He'd fearlessly taken on the world.

Now a tube snaked obscenely from his throat to a machine that I knew was breathing for him. Wires dangled from his chest and led to monitors. Another tube ran from an IV bag to his hand.

I could hardly see Gray underneath it all.

"It is a shock to see someone you love like this," the nurse said kindly. "But it helps to remember that all this equipment is helping him."

For months, we'd lived apart. I'd gone days, even weeks, without seeing him or talking to him. Now, I'd give anything if he'd open his eyes and say my name. Just *Addie*. For a man who didn't articulate much, he had a way of infusing just my name with so much . . . well, love. But more than that. When he said my name I felt his belief in me. I remembered so many moments when that one word had told me so much.

"Ma'am?" the nurse said.

I realized that I'd been ready to dive into a memory again. I forced myself to concentrate on the present. "The doctor said he could be like this for a while?"

"Yes. Probably days. The doctors want to make sure his blood pressure is down and under control before they let him wake up."

"Because of the tear and the stent?" In the here and now, I felt as if I were trying to wade through mud. I felt as if I couldn't hold on to the information they were telling me.

But I slipped into the past with ease and reveled in the moments I shared with Gray. Moments I'd almost forgotten about in the pain of the last year were suddenly crystal clear.

For months, there was one moment with Gray that stood in the forefront of my mind. It was the straw that broke our marriage's back. I'd come to think of it as my *straw moment*. I thought about it a lot and I hadn't been able to get past it enough to look back at some of our better moments.

Until today.

Until it could be too late.

"Your husband," she said, as if she could sense my thoughts and wanted to remind me Gray was still my husband, "will be sedated until he's stronger and more stable. The longer he goes on, the better his odds."

She didn't say *goes on* what. I knew she meant the longer he continued breathing—went on living—the better his odds were of surviving.

I nodded.

"You can sit with him until eight o'clock," she continued. "Then we ask the families to go home and get some rest. You can come back in the morning refreshed and better able to cope with everything."

I looked at the clock. It was after four.

I'd lost all track of time here.

I had imagined that by now I'd have given Gray the papers and he'd have signed them. His signing the papers wouldn't be enough to make our divorce official, but it would have been a symbolic end for me.

And a new beginning.

I'd thought by now I'd be sitting on the deck, watching the sun begin to set on my old life. I thought I'd be sipping a glass of wine and dreaming about what the next chapter of my life would look like.

I hadn't been able to figure out what I wanted that future to be, but I knew that the last year wasn't it.

"Mrs. Grayson, are you sure you're okay?" the nurse asked.

I nodded.

Mrs. Grayson.

The words felt like a lie, but I didn't say that. I said, "Thank you," just as I had other times today.

"You can talk to him," she said. "He's under sedation, but he will hear you. He'll know you're here."

I was relieved when she left to go to her perch just outside the door.

The ICU rooms were like the spokes in a wheel. From her station the nurse could see her patients, monitor their vitals, and was never more than a handful of steps away from any one of them.

This was where they sent the most touch-and-go patients.

This is where they sent the patients who were fighting for their lives.

After a day surrounded by people and noise as I waited for news about Gray, the quiet sounds of this room felt disconcerting. The faint hum of the machines. The soft whoosh of the ventilator. The muted noises from the rest of the hospital.

I looked out the long, narrow window. It wasn't much of a window, but it was something. After spending much of the day in windowless rooms, I felt a small tremor of surprise that the world still seemed to be going on at its regular pace. Cars still sped along the city streets. The clouds obscured the sun, but I knew it was on its way down. The days were shorter in October.

People still went about their day.

Working. Playing. Laughing.

JoAnn was probably still at the store, covering for me.

Ash was probably still at his office, wheeling and dealing.

Everyone was simply going along with the tasks at hand.

My tasks had narrowed to just one. Gray.

He was the only thing on my agenda and there was really nothing I could do but wait.

I was here in limbo . . . just waiting. Along with Maude, James, and Harriet.

Waiting to see if our loved ones recovered. Knowing there was nothing else we could do for them.

"Here I am," I said simply to Gray. "I'm here for you."

After months of not talking, those words said it all.

Our relationship was damaged, maybe irreparably broken, but I was here for him.

I didn't hold his hand because of the IV in it, but I laid my hand lightly on his fingertips, reminding him that he wasn't alone.

I tried to think of something else to say, but couldn't, so I slipped into silence.

The light whir of the machines was a white noise. It was easy to be lulled by the sound. Occasionally the intercom squawked, pulling me from my almost trance, but as soon as it silenced, I let myself fall back into the hum.

The nurse came in on occasion and looked at the machines. Once she shifted Gray on the bed, propping him on his side with pillows. "We want to prevent sores, so we'll change his position for him."

I nodded.

"Visiting hours are over in a half hour," she said.

"Thank you," I replied because I wasn't sure what else to say. I'd stopped counting how many times I'd said those two words by rote, not meaning them at all.

"They're going to make me leave soon," I said to him. "But I'll be back in the morning."

I pulled out the picture and swan that I'd taken from Gray's office and set them on the stand next to his bed.

I stared at the old photo. "We were so happy then. Where did we go wrong?" I asked myself . . . or maybe him.

I still had my swan at the Ferncliff house, tucked away in my jewelry box.

I'd seen him take his that night, but I hadn't seen it since. Why had he found it and brought it out now? On his desk next to that picture?

I looked at Gray in the picture, then back at him on the bed, hooked up to tubes and wires.

The nurse sat just outside the room, presumably checking the monitors, ready to spring into action if anything happened.

I pulled the chair right up to the side of the bed and slid my hand under his, so I didn't disturb the IV. It felt dry and cool.

I whispered, "I know I could live my life on my own . . . I've proven it over these last months. But, Gray, I don't know if I can live my life on my own if you're gone. I've been so mad at you. You let me mourn alone and then you let me go. But I can't let you go. I won't."

I don't know how long I sat there, holding his hand, but the next thing I knew, the nurse was touching my shoulders. "Visiting hours are over."

I nodded and wordlessly rose. I realized I was still holding Gray's hand. I kissed his fingertips. "I'll be back first thing."

I gathered my purse and the stupid envelope. I stopped at the nurses' station. "I think I gave all my information when I registered Gray, but to be honest, I'm not sure. I wanted to be sure you had my cell number. You'll call me if there's any change?"

She took the card I extended to her. "I'll check that it's in the system, and I promise we'll call if there's any change."

I looked back at Gray before leaving. I don't think I've ever walked so slowly.

I didn't know where to go.

Ferncliff? Glenwood? I knew the phone reception was spotty at the Ferncliff house. That fact hadn't bothered me before, but I needed to be sure the hospital could reach me.

I knew that Gray wouldn't mind if I went to the house on Willow Lane, but I wasn't sure I could face it.

I started to walk toward the elevator, still not sure where I was going to go, but needing to move.

"Addie?" someone said. I jumped at the sound of my name. It seemed to reverberate in the empty hall.

I spun around and found Ash sitting in a small bank of chairs across from the elevators. "Ash?"

I didn't need to ask why he was here.

His face was pinched with worry.

Ash, the eternal optimist, was worried.

He always believed the world was a wonderful place. And why shouldn't he? He came from an affluent, loving family. He'd met Gray in college and they'd meshed. They were more than friends from the beginning. They were brothers. They'd built a successful business before either had reached their thirties.

Ash was the other half of Gray in a way I'd never be.

"They said I wasn't family, so I couldn't go back," Ash said. He sounded mystified that the hospital wouldn't deem him family.

"You should have said you were his brother. We both know that's the truth. Or you could have had the nurse tell me you were here. I would have come out and talked to them."

"No. I saw you sitting with him and knew you were what he needed. You've always been what he needed, Addie."

I snorted at that.

Ash beckoned me to sit down and I obliged, more because I wasn't ready to leave the hospital than because I needed to hear Ash's pep talk. I could see him forming his rah-rah comments as I sat there. "I know you two are going through a rough patch—"

I stopped him by thrusting the now-ragged-looking manila envelope at him.

"I was at his office today bringing him these." Ash held the envelope as if he didn't know what to do with it, so I said, "Go ahead, open it."

He opened the envelope and pulled out the papers. "Divorce?"

"We're well past the point of no return. I thought it was time. I asked for half our savings, my car, and my personal items, but everything else is Gray's. The house. His stake in the company. I would never interfere with something you two worked so hard to build."

"You're entitled to part of it." Ash said the words I'd thought Gray would say. I know the image for businessmen is greed, but that wasn't the case with either Ash or Gray. They might have different personal styles, but they both had honor that was bone deep.

I liked to think that so did I. I shook my head. "No. The company is his and yours."

Suddenly, Ash's expression hardened. "So you gave him the papers and he had a heart attack?"

I shook my head. "No. He never saw the papers."

I could see that moment so clearly. Gray had looked unsure, but happy to see me. And then he'd collapsed in pain. So much pain. And I'd been helpless to stop it.

Ash still eyed me suspiciously. "You can't give them to him now."

"No. Not now," I assured him. "Ash, I'm just not sure where we'll go when he's well. It's been almost a year."

"No, it hasn't," Ash said, echoing JoAnn. "It's been eight months since you walked out. Gray would probably be able to tell you how many weeks and days, but eight months is accurate enough. A year isn't."

I refused to quibble about how long it had been since I left Gray, because, truth be told, he'd left me long before I walked out that door. "Regardless, it's over. Until this morning, I hadn't seen him for weeks. And last time I did see him, it didn't go well."

I braced myself for Ash to say something hurtful, but instead he simply said, "Addie, he needs you."

"Right now, yes. But when he's better?" I shook my head.

"He loves you," Ash insisted.

"Maybe in his way, but I don't think his way is the way I need to be loved." I didn't need someone who babbled about every little thing, but I did need someone who talked. Who shared something of himself.

Ash didn't try to argue my comment; instead he asked, "Do you remember your first date?"

We'd been friends for so many years, and slowly we'd become something more, though neither of us had admitted it. We'd gone together to our senior prom and I'd thought something might happen, but nothing had. Not until . . .

I thought about the swan that had been sitting in his office. Its twin still tucked up in my jewelry box at home. "Of course," I said quietly.

"Gray and I were assigned as roommates. And we hardly knew each other, but he came in that night with some stupid plastic thing and set it down on the windowsill in front of his desk. *What the hell is that?* I asked.

"*A reminder*, he said. Addie, he looked at me and was so serious when he said, *It's a reminder of what I'm working toward.* Then he smiled at me. I think it's the first time I ever saw him really smile."

"I used to tease him that he was a smile hoarder," I said. And sometimes when I teased him about it, he'd smile.

"Yeah. Well, after that date when he came in so happy, I was a bit freaked out," Ash said. "And I said something like *What did you do tonight?* He said, *I went out with the woman I'm going to marry.*"

I knew that Ash had to be rewriting history. "No, he didn't. I wasn't sure there'd be a second date. We both worried about how it would affect our friendship."

"Yes, he did. He said he'd gone out with you and I said something about him knowing you all his life, but he clarified, *Since the first day of kindergarten.* As if he wanted me to be clear on it. As if he regretted those first five years he didn't know you.

"Then he said something like *I didn't know I was going to marry her until tonight. We sat at the table together and I put my arm around her. And I thought, I could spend the rest of my life listening to her and holding her. That's when I realized I loved her.*" Ash paused a moment, then added, "He said he thought he'd always loved you."

Ash stuffed the papers back into the envelope and handed it to me. "He'll never sign them."

I couldn't imagine Gray saying any of those things. Maybe Ash saw my skepticism, because he nodded. "The thing about Gray is, he doesn't say much, so when he does say something, people pay attention. I'm pretty sure I'm close to perfect on what he said. He loved you. He still does. And he'll never sign those," Ash said with complete conviction.

His utter certainty shook my own.

"Gray's a man who likes things orderly," I said hesitantly. "He'll see the logic in divorcing now when we might go back to being friends."

When I'd talked to JoAnn this morning, I'd believed that. But now? I wasn't so sure of Gray's reaction, and I was even less sure about what I wanted.

"You were never his friend. You were—are—the love of his life." Ash got up and said, "Were you going home?"

I still didn't know which place to go to. Neither felt right. "No. I'm staying for a while longer."

"You'll call me if you need anything? If anything changes?"

I nodded.

"Did he really say all those things?" I asked, needing to hear Gray's words, even if they were coming from Ash.

Ash nodded. "Addie, I know it's been a rough year and I'm so sorry for everything . . ." He stopped as if he didn't know what else to say.

Most people didn't know what to say about what happened.

Not even Gray.

Ash continued, ". . . but you should know, it took everything Gray had not to come after you. He was giving you time and space, but he never stopped loving you, and he never stopped believing you two would find your way to the other side."

"I did find my way to the other side," I said simply, not that there was anything simple between the two of us. I found my way to other side and discovered it didn't include Gray.

Ash started to walk to the elevator and then turned around. "He's started listening to Broadway."

"Pardon?" Gray listening to Broadway tunes sounded implausible at best.

I had season tickets to Erie's Broadway series. Most of the time I took JoAnn. But when she couldn't go, I dragged Gray with me, kicking and screaming.

"Broadway tunes?" I repeated, sure I must have heard wrong.

"Yes. It kinda freaks me and the staff out. He said you sing songs from your favorite shows a lot and he missed them. So he plays them." He paused a moment then added, "And he said you taught him that sometimes the music can say things more eloquently than words. I don't know what those show tunes were saying, but I just thought you should know."

"Thanks," I said, not sure what I was going to do with that information.

"Call me," Ash said as he got on the elevator.

"Yes."

I tried to imagine Gray listening to Broadway musicals, and it just seemed too incongruous. He was not a music fan. He didn't turn on the radio for background noise. He didn't even turn it on when he was driving.

He never seemed to mind when I did, but I don't think he'd have ever done so on his own.

I felt odd sitting in what was nothing more than a nook in a hallway, so I got up and thought I'd go get some coffee.

As I got off the elevator and turned toward the cafeteria, I realized I didn't want coffee.

I saw the double doors of the chapel I'd noticed earlier.

No one would notice just one more person sitting in there. So I made a beeline.

There was only one other person in the room. Her hair was like an announcement—*look at me*, the fire-engine color said.

The rest of her said, *don't look*. She had on black yoga pants, an oversize sweatshirt, and UGGs. Her head was bent, so her hair spilled over her shoulders, shrouding her face.

I sat behind her, trying to give her space. I thought about Gray listening to Broadway tunes and tried to have that make sense.

Suddenly her shoulders heaved and she made a quiet, low, keening sound.

I reached out and started to put my hand on her shoulder, then thought better of it. Instead, I said, "Are you all right?"

She sat up and turned around. I realized that she was my age . . . maybe a little younger, but she was somewhere in those ambiguous years between youth and middle age.

She wiped at her eyes and nodded. We both knew it was a lie.

"Okay then," I said, not wanting to intrude.

I sank back in my seat and she surprised me—surprised herself as well, if her expression was any indication—by saying, "How do you miss someone you hardly know?"

"I'm not sure," I said. The utter longing in her voice reminded me of my own longing. I'm not sure I recognized how much I missed Gray until now, until I had no way of reaching him.

"I don't know her. My mother. My birth mother. And he said—her husband—he said that they'd been waiting for me. I believed him, but I thought it was waiting like waiting for your vacation, or even like a kid who's waiting for Christmas. I thought she was looking forward to meeting me someday. But that's not it. She wrote this"—she held out a worn leather journal—"and when I read it, I can feel her . . . *aching*. That's the word. She was *aching* with the waiting."

Her hand went to the locket around her neck. She clasped it tightly, as if it were a lifeline. "I occasionally thought about finding her, you know. But I put it off. I knew I'd look for her someday . . . but life got in the way. And she was out here waiting for me. Aching."

I understood what she was saying today more than I would have understood it yesterday.

I said, "I thought earlier that maybe the word *waiting* comes from the word *weight*. I thought I'd be crushed under the weight of my waiting."

She nodded, her hair undulating as she did. "Yes. I can feel her aching under the weight of it on every page. Now the tables are turned and I'm the one who's waiting . . . aching under the weight of it all."

"This is not a normal conversation for two strangers." I didn't mean to say the words out loud, but I was pretty sure this woman realized it as well. I thought about Maude, James, and Harriet. "I think that everyone here who's waiting has a common bond. It means none of us are strangers, even if we've never met before. I'm Addie."

"I'm Siobhan. Who are you waiting for?" she asked.

I was getting better at answering this question. "My husband."

The designation came out with more assurance than it had earlier in the day.

Gray was my husband. That wasn't going to change anytime soon.

"He had heart surgery today," I added. "They kicked me out of ICU and told me to go home for the night, but I couldn't."

"My . . . I don't know what to call her. *Mother* isn't right. I had a mother who loved me and raised me. A mother I adored. But *birth mother* seems too formal. Everyone else calls her Piper or Pip, but she's more than that to me." She shrugged.

"Maybe giving her a name doesn't matter. It's hard to watch someone you love suffering."

"I've only just met her. How can I love her? How can I love any of them?" she asked.

I thought of that moment I found out I was pregnant. In that instant, I was in love. "Sometimes love comes quickly, sometimes more slowly. Real love comes in its own time."

Siobhan nodded. "She always loved me. It's on every page. Every single one of them. She built a life around me and loved me. Every day of my life, she loved me so much. How could I not have felt it? Even not knowing her, how can someone be loved that much and not be aware of it?"

I thought of Gray and answered, "I don't know. You're right, it seems as if that kind of love should be palpable. And maybe if someone loves you that much, it's hard not to love them in return."

A man came into the chapel. "Siobhan?"

"Logan, is she okay?" my new friend asked.

"She's fine."

Siobhan stood up, clutching the worn leather book to her chest. "I hope your husband's okay."

I took her hand and squeezed it. "I hope *she* is as well." I didn't refer to the woman in question as Siobhan's mother, or her birth mother. She had to make her own decision about what their relationship was.

She noticed and smiled her thanks, then rushed out of the chapel with the man.

Siobhan had clutched the book and I realized I was holding the envelope just as tightly. I couldn't read it and find comfort in the pages, as she'd been doing. These pages were filled with regret that love sometimes wasn't enough.

Once, I'd thought it would be.

And yet, I'd so blithely assured Siobhan that love came in its own time. And that maybe when someone loved you that much, it was palpable. Her birth mother had filled a notebook with words, describing her love.

Gray would never have the words for something like that.

He'd told me as much once.

I knew exactly what day it was.

We'd just officially bought the house. The closing was right before the end of the business day, so we couldn't move in that day, but Gray—being Gray—was prepared.

He'd bought an air mattress, and Peggy had packed another picnic. Keys in hand, we'd let ourselves into the house. We'd toured it again, and I'd talked about my plans for each room while Gray listened and nodded. He'd built a fire and we had our dinner in front of the fire.

And then . . .

Memories of the first time we'd made love in that house threatened to overwhelm me. And I realized that while I loved the house on Willow Lane, and even the house on Ferncliff, the only place I'd ever felt truly at home was in Gray's arms.

Afterward, on that air mattress in front of the fireplace . . .

"I'm so utterly content right now," I murmured as I slid a millimeter closer to him. I wanted to obliterate any separation. I wanted to hold on to him—to this moment—forever. "This is how we should spend the rest of our lives."

Gray grinned at my words and I didn't need him to say anything to know that he was teasing me. In his head, he was being literal, thinking we should be naked in front of the fireplace for the rest of our lives.

As if to confirm I was right, he quirked an eyebrow, inviting me to stay this way a bit longer.

Someone else might miss that he was teasing, but I recognized the signs.

I shoved him. "Be serious."

"I am" was all he'd said as he brushed some imaginary hair back from my cheek. And he'd pulled me back into his arms. "I'll never be able to put things into words as easily as you, but Addie, I'm . . ."

He paused.

I waited.

I knew he wouldn't spout an epic poem to describe how he felt, but I didn't need epic.

". . . happy," he'd finally finished.

I snuggled even closer. No epic poem had ever put it so sweetly. I tried to imprint that moment in my memory, knowing that I never wanted to forget it.

Even though I'd tried to hold on to that moment, I'd forgotten.

Until now. Until it could be too late.

How had I forgotten all the moments I'd remembered so freely today? How had I let one horrible moment obscure them?

I thought about that same man a few floors away from me.

I wondered what else I'd forgotten.

Chapter Eight

After Siobhan left, no one else came into the chapel. After a day spent with people, all of them suffering under the weight of their waiting, the quiet solitude was a balm.

There was no hum of machines. No nurses popping in and bustling about. No doctors looking serious.

I couldn't hear call bells or PA announcements.

I'd spent the day delving into the past, remembering what Gray and I once had. Though I could remember those moments clearly again now, I wasn't sure we could ever get back to that easier, happier point in our relationship. There was no going back.

And it was hard to look to the future with his life still hanging by a thread.

For a long time, I sat in silence, simply trying to live in the here and now.

Here and now, Gray was alive and recuperating a few floors away.

Here and now, the divorce papers were still in my hand, unsigned.

So here and now, I was still his wife.

But keeping myself in the here and now was difficult. Try as I might, the past kept tumbling into my thoughts, intermingling with fears of the future.

I'd spent the last eight months unable to look backward and hating to look forward.

Live in the now. I'd heard that advice or variations of it for years, but how can you live in the present without the certainty of the past and the possibility of the future?

It felt as if I'd spent the past months at Ferncliff in limbo.

In the quiet chapel, I worked to sit silently in the present.

I was here.

Gray was still here.

I started to shove the envelope back in my purse, but it seemed like too much effort so I let it fall to my lap.

For just a moment, I let the past and present take care of themselves, and I stilled. I settled into that one moment and found my respite. Slowly, even the muted sounds of the hospital faded. There was just that moment. One breath after another.

No past pulling at me. No present intruding.

I was here. Gray was just a few floors up.

I was his wife.

He was my husband.

I'm not sure how long I sat in the quiet chapel, pushing all thoughts and worries aside. Having them creep back in, then pushing them away again.

It became a rhythm like my breathing.

In and out.

Out and in.

I lost track of time. I'd almost forgotten about the world that bustled along beyond this room's walls.

But the respite couldn't last.

"You've been here a long time," a male voice said quietly from behind me.

He hadn't been quiet enough not to make me jump.

He looked apologetic. "I don't want to interrupt your prayers, but I wondered if I could sit with you?"

He was a young man in well-worn jeans and an Erie Otters T-shirt.

"I'm not praying," I admitted. "I've always thought it seemed disingenuous to ignore God until the moment that you needed him, then show up, hat in hand, on his doorstep, begging for favors."

"I'm Mark, the chaplain here," he said. "Though I guess tonight, I'm more of a visitor."

He didn't look old enough to be a chaplain, but I didn't say that. I simply asked, "What time is it?"

"After ten." He pulled his phone out of his pocket and checked the time. "Ten thirty-one, to be precise."

"You were right. I've been here a long time." I'd been at the hospital for less than a day. It seemed like more.

So much more.

"You're at the hospital for a relative?" he asked.

"My husband," I said. The envelope that would have changed that sat heavily on my lap, but I didn't let it change my answer. "I'm here for my husband."

"Sometimes sharing your worries eases your burdens," he said as an invitation to speak. "We can say a lot in our silences, but with people there always comes a time for the silence to end. There comes a time when the words need to be said. If it's that time for you, I'm here."

I didn't know whether to laugh or cry at his words. I'd never minded Gray's quiet nature. Ash was right; Gray didn't say much, but when he did say something, everyone paid attention.

I'd always felt I could hear the words he didn't say. And he always said I talked enough for both of us. Remembering that made me smile.

But remembering the time I needed him to say something, and the words he'd said . . .

I shook my head.

Maybe. It's. For. The. Best.

The words seemed heavier than ever.

Those words had haunted me ever since.

I pushed that memory aside and held out my hand. "Hi, Mark. I'm Addie."

"And you're here with your husband?"

I nodded and gave the envelope a twist. Then I shook my head. "Yes, my husband now, but when he collapsed I was going to put a formal end to our marriage," I finally said.

He didn't need to ask his questions; they were all right there in that one slightly raised eyebrow.

I slid the envelope to Mark. "I went to see him today to give him these."

He cocked his head, asking permission to look inside the envelope. I nodded. He saw what the papers were and put the flap back in place, then handed me back the envelope.

"And yet, you're still here?" he said.

"They're strict on visiting hours in ICU. I understand their policy, but I can't leave. I don't know where to go," I admitted and immediately felt embarrassed by the confession.

"Do you live together?"

"I left him . . ." Normally I'd say *a year ago*, because knowing the real answer seemed pathetic. But I didn't think Mark would judge me. "Eight months ago."

I remembered what Ash had said about Gray and did the math, then corrected myself. "Eight months and thirteen days ago."

"Because you fell out of love with him?"

Someone asking me such personal, pointed questions would normally make my hackles rise, but Mark wasn't pushy. It didn't feel as if he was asking to be nosy, but rather because he really wanted to hear my answer.

I didn't need to think about it. I shook my head. "No. Not that."

"Because he fell out of love with you?" he asked.

Again, I shook my head. "No. No, I don't think so."

"I'm at a loss then." And that's exactly how he looked . . . as if he couldn't fathom why I'd leave a relationship with someone I still loved.

"Maybe that's just it. We were both lost and neither of us knew what to say in order to find our way back to the way we used to be."

"Sometimes words can't really convey our true meaning. Sometimes the words we don't say are the ones that matter the most," Mark reiterated. "I think it's kind of like that with praying. It's not disingenuous to say *here I am*. Just those three words."

"I'm not sure."

"It's not the words that matter, it's the intention behind them. The feelings, even. Three words—*here I am*. Those and three other words are the ones that matter the most, I think."

"What are the other three?" I found myself asking.

"I love you."

I studied this kid and said, "You're an odd minister."

Mark laughed at that. "I'm a hockey fan, a farmer, and . . . yes, an odd minister. That's a big compliment. Thank you."

I laughed as well. It was rusty and small, but it was there. "You're welcome."

"You're planning to spend the night in here?"

I nodded. "I could go back to our house, or to the house I've been living in, but I can't be that far away from him. I spent almost a year—"

"Eight months and thirteen days," he filled in.

I nodded. "I thought I could spend the rest of my life that far away from him, but I was wrong. So I'll just wait here until visiting hours in the morning."

"You know, I don't have a lot of clout anywhere, but I think I have enough here that I can help you out. Hang on."

He left me again.

I'd never thought about it before, but now that I did, I thought he was right.

I simply had to trust and say, "Here I am."

And maybe, "Thank you."

That was it. Whatever happened, I could give thanks. Thanks for all the love I had for Gray, because no matter what had happened, that love was still there. Maybe I'd thought it was gone. But it wasn't. I'd only misplaced it . . . pushed it aside and let my pain and my anger obscure it.

Here I am and *I love you.* According to Mark, those words mattered most.

I looked at the envelope in my hand. The papers in it were full of words, but maybe none of them really came to much in the end.

"Come with me," Mark said. He led me back to the fourth floor and to Gray's room. "This is Alice" was his introduction of a tiny, brown-haired nurse.

"I would have been here to meet you before you left, but we had a bit of a crisis at home," she said.

"Everything okay?" Mark asked, looking concerned.

"Fine." She looked at me. "The kids do keep life interesting."

Mark didn't look completely convinced, but he said, "Alice is the night nurse. And she's got this horrible vision problem, which probably explains why she can't see you when you sit very still in your husband's room."

She smiled again. "I'd say it's nice to meet you, but I can't see you at all. Probably because I left a pillow and blanket on the chair, and you're going to cover up, close your eyes, and get some sleep. So, I won't notice you until right before shift change, when I'll finally see you and wake you. Then you can go grab some breakfast before the official visiting hours start."

I looked at the two of them. "Thank you," I said.

Maude, James, Harriet, Siobhan, and now Mark and Alice. My day had been touched by so many people, and since I couldn't thank the rest of them, I settled for repeating "Thank you" to Mark and Alice.

She nodded. "I took a look at your husband's chart. He does better when you're here."

"Really?"

She nodded. "According to the numbers, after visiting hours, his blood pressure was elevated, along with his heart rate. I'm sure the daytime nurses have explained that this isn't really a coma. The doctors are giving him drugs that keep him sedated until we get his blood pressure under control. But he can hear you. He can sense you. And when you're nearby, he's calmer. That's good for his recovery."

Gray knew I was here.

There was a comfort in that knowledge.

Alice was right, the other nurses had said as much, but I thought it was just something they said to patients' families.

"All those things you've wanted to say to him . . . now is your chance," Mark said. "So get some sleep and think about what you want to tell your husband."

I looked at this young man who possessed a very old soul. "Thank you. I'm not sure why you were at the chapel so late, but I'm glad you were."

"My father . . ." he started then stopped.

"He's a patient?"

Mark nodded. "I thought that maybe being sick would soften him, but it didn't."

"According to a new friend, there are two sets of words that really matter. *Here I am* and *I love you.*"

"I hate it when my sage advice comes back to bite me," he said now with vehemence. He turned to leave. "Would it be okay if I stopped in to check on you and your husband?"

"I would really welcome that."

Mark left, and I could hear him having a whispered conversation with Alice outside Gray's room.

I put the envelope and my purse down, slid the chair right next to Gray's bed, and reached out and took his hand.

"I still don't know what to say to you, but *here I am*," I told him as I stroked his palm with my forefinger. "I'm not going anywhere, so you just sleep. I'll stay here with you."

I reclined the chair and turned my head toward Gray, propping it on the pillow. "I found our picture and the plastic swan on your desk. I brought them here. They're on the nightstand," I whispered.

"I still have my swan, too. It's in my jewelry box. I should probably move it somewhere else because I could handle it if someone stole all my jewelry, but I'd be heartbroken if they took that."

I pushed thoughts of the past I couldn't change out of my mind and refused to look into the future. Right now, I was here, holding Gray's hand.

The doctor had said the longer he survived, the better his chances.

Every tick of the clock meant he was that much further along the road to recovery.

That was enough for now.

Chapter Nine

I woke with a start and was confused by the cacophony of strange sounds. For half a second, I couldn't remember where I was. And then I saw Gray, and everything that had happened yesterday came rushing back.

I sat up straight, which dislodged my hand from Gray's. Numb from hours of being in an awkward position, it fell with a thud to the arm of the chair. I picked it up with my other hand and began to rub my palm.

Harmon was standing on the other side of Gray's bed, typing something on his phone.

"Harmon?"

"I'm sorry. I didn't mean to wake you. I promised Jo that I'd check on you, but even without her nudging, I'd have stopped by. Do you need anything?"

I didn't know this Harmon, in his white doctor's lab coat over his powder-blue scrubs. The Harmon I knew was a man who wore jeans and old T-shirts. A man who seemed as at home with a baby on his hip as he did with his arm casually slung over JoAnn's shoulder.

"You look like a real doctor," I said, still half asleep. "Sorry, I mean, I know you are, but I don't ever see you like this."

"Well, if anyone here asks, your story is I'm a serious doctor, even at home."

I smiled. "Sure. I can lie for you."

Harmon laughed, then turned serious as he looked at Gray. "I checked and want to reassure you that even if it really doesn't seem like it, he's doing okay. I—"

Harmon's cell phone rang. He pulled it from his lab coat pocket. "Pardon me." He turned. "Yes." Pause. "That's great." Pause. "You're just doing this to get even with me." Pause. He sighed. "No, I'm not with a patient. I'm with Addie."

He turned to me. "It's Jo. She wants me to put her on speaker." He shrugged apologetically.

"Addie, I'll be over later," JoAnn's disembodied voice said. "Sorry to interrupt, but Wills made me call Harmon. Go for it."

Harmon sighed again and then mouthed the words *I'm so sorry* before he sang, "Everybody poops. Everybody pees. All the animals, Mommy, and me. So come on, Wills, and poop with me."

I don't think he was aware of the fact, but he had a bit of swaying going on as he sang, as if at home he actually did a dance but he was trying to contain it here.

I couldn't help it; I laughed.

"Hey, Wills, do you want Aunt Addie to sing with me?" he asked, grinning at me.

Three more rounds of the song and Jo informed us that mission was accomplished.

I was still laughing as Harmon hung up.

"Thank you," I said. "Believe it or not, that was just what I needed."

"Tell you what, if I get another emergency call from home, I'll come back up. We had a good duet going."

"Gee, Harmon, you're so good to me."

"And don't forget, your job, if you're asked, is to confirm my total and serious doctorness. And you must never reveal my potty-singing ways."

I smiled and made a cross-my-heart sign over my chest.

I don't think Harmon realized that he was humming the tune as he walked back out of the room.

I looked at the machines that Gray was hooked up to. Maybe I couldn't read them the way Harmon could, but I could see his heart rate. It beat steadily, and even I knew that had to be a good thing.

"Harmon says you're okay, Gray," I said.

It was still dark out, so I lay back in the chair and asked my husband, "As I was singing with Harmon I realized that you would have been like that. Despite the fact most people would find it hard to believe, you would have stopped an important meeting to sing a potty song to our baby."

I took his hand in mine.

I must have fallen back to sleep because the next thing I was aware of was Nurse Alice writing on Gray's chart. I realized I still held his hand in mine.

"Sorry," she said apologetically. "I'm glad you got some sleep."

"How is he?" I asked, cradling my numb hand, feeling the first pricks of needles as blood began flowing.

"Stable," she assured me in a quiet voice.

"Is he out of the woods?" I gave my hand a small shake and was rewarded by a thousand pinpricks.

I ignored the feeling and concentrated on Nurse Alice. She gave me a small, reassuring smile as she said, "Not yet, but every hour that goes by is another step in the right direction."

She fiddled with a machine while I continued shaking the life back into my hand.

Satisfied with whatever she'd read, she said, "The morning shift will be starting in an hour. Why don't you run home, take a shower, and grab some breakfast? You'll feel better for it. You can't take care of him if you don't take care of yourself. I know that sometimes we all forget that."

"Pot calling the kettle black?" I asked.

She nodded. "You don't know the half of it. Between work and family I rarely have any time to call my own. Well, other than a few minutes each morning."

"What happens in the morning?"

"I go down to the coffee shop in the lobby and get one small black coffee, then take a few minutes to just drink it." She looked at me with a conspiratorial grin. "And sometimes if I'm being really wild, I get a medium rather than the small."

Despite everything I couldn't help but laugh. I laughed easier now than I had in months. "You are wild."

"Thank you for noticing." She looked pleased with her *wild* status. "Go home, shower, and get breakfast. And some coffee."

"I'll make it a medium and think of you," I promised her.

I stood up and started to fold the blanket I'd used while I thought about taking care of Gray when he was released from the hospital. "There's very little chance Gray will let me take care of him, you know. He likes to be the one doing the caring, not vice versa."

"That will have to change," she assured me. "He's going to need care. When he's able, he'll need some rehab, and when he goes home he'll have to think about restructuring his life. And it doesn't sound like that will be easy for him."

"Restructure how?" I put the pillow and blanket on the windowsill.

"Controlling his blood pressure will be imperative. Medication will be part of it, but it will require a lifestyle change as well."

I picked up my purse and the now-well-mutilated envelope. "He'll have limitations?"

"He won't be running any marathons, but he should be able to have a normal life. But he'll have to find time to relax." Alice smiled again. She was one of those people who seemed to send off calming, it's-all-going-to-be-okay vibes. I wondered if she'd always had that sort of aura, or if working as a nurse had made her that way.

It didn't matter how she came by it, I leaned on her calm confidence. Gray would be okay and have a normal life.

And needed to relax. "If Gray were writing the dictionary, *relax* would be a four-letter word."

Nurse Alice tucked the sheet more securely around my husband. "He's going to have to learn. How about yoga? In the summer, there's a group that meets on Presque Isle at sunset. I've always thought it would be fun. Maybe if you went, you could entice him. A long vacation on a beach with nothing to do each day but watch the sun rise and then set."

I didn't comment on the irony of that comment. A beach vacation had been the straw moment for me.

We'd lost our way in December and had limped along for weeks. I'd resolved to try one last time.

I'd called Missy and made sure the week was clear for Gray . . . well, as clear as any week was for him. Then I talked to Ash, who readily agreed to fill in for Gray. With the two of them on board, I put the tickets on hold and waited. Hoping beyond hope that if we could just get away, we could find our way back to us . . .

I heard Gray's car pull into the garage. I'd been waiting for him.

I was nervous. Gray wasn't someone who enjoyed surprises, but I was hoping that just as he'd once surprised me with the house, he'd like my plans for us. After two aborted attempts at a honeymoon and more than a dozen discussions about possibly getting away, I'd put a hold on the perfect honeymoon. The perfect getaway where we could rediscover who we were as a couple.

Gray walked into the kitchen and eyed me warily. "You look better."

I nodded. "I feel better." I wasn't sure if that was the truth, but maybe if I said it often enough, I'd eventually believe it.

"I have a surprise for you." I slid our itinerary across the counter.

Gray picked it up and examined it. "St. Lucia?"

I nodded. "It's an all-inclusive resort. I went to an actual travel agent. She's got it all ready. It's not a long flight, but it's far enough away to make it feel like a real honeymoon. Everything's included. There's a list of excursions we can take if you like, but I'd be happy with nothing more than being with you. We can take long walks on the beach, hang out at the pool. I just have to call her . . ."

My sentence faded as I saw his expression.

He set the paper down. "Addie, you should have talked to me about this. I can't get away right now—"

"You can. Missy was careful about your schedule. And Ash said he'd fill in—"

He hadn't touched me since we'd lost the baby and when he finally reached for me, it wasn't a warm embrace. Instead, he held my shoulders and looked me in the eye. "I can't."

Those two words were inaccurate. He should have said, I won't.

But accurate or not, they were the straw that broke the camel's back.

I knew even as I made the decision that I'd never confess to anyone that this was my reason for leaving. It sounded frivolous and foolish.

Here he was, touching me for the first time in months only to push me away . . . again.

I needed him so much after we lost our son, and he'd turned away. I kept waiting for him to turn back, but he hadn't.

"Addie, I'm sorry," he said, "but I can't."

"All right," I said softly. I thought about packing, but in the end, I kissed his cheek, picked up my purse, and walked out to the garage.

"Good-bye, Gray." That's all I said.

He didn't follow me.

I got in the car and backed out of the drive. I called Jo and asked if I could stay at her Ferncliff house.

She said yes, just as I knew she would.

I walked away from the man I loved because I was afraid that if I stayed, I'd eventually hate him.

❧ ❧ ❧

I had never minded how much Gray loved his work. Oh, I hadn't enjoyed the times we'd planned a getaway and he'd canceled, but I understood.

Maybe I should have told him more clearly that this wasn't some whim. It wasn't even really an attempt to finally go on the honeymoon we'd never had.

It was a lifeline that I was throwing to us as a couple. A lifeline I threw and clung to.

A lifeline he simply ignored.

After I'd left Gray, I'd Googled the phrase *the straw that broke the camel's back*. I couldn't find any definitive answer as to where the phrase originated. A few sites pointed to a saying about *the last feather that broke the horse's back*, or about *the last drop of coffee that overflowed the cup*.

In the end, I decided it didn't matter. They all dealt with that one last, frequently tiny, thing that made something difficult become something impossible.

Leaving because he wouldn't go on vacation with me sounded ridiculous, but it was my straw moment.

I realized that Nurse Alice was still in the room as I stared at my husband, remembering that one last time.

"You'll be heading home for that breakfast and shower, right?" she asked.

"Yes," I promised. "I'll just say good-bye."

She started to leave the room, then turned around. "Addie, I work again tonight if you want to stay."

"Thank you." I felt my eyes well up by this unexpected small kindness. "I mean it, thank you."

"I can see how much you love him. Being surrounded by that kind of love can only help him."

She left me alone with my husband, her words ringing in my ears.

I remembered yesterday morning—was it only yesterday?—sitting on the deck with my cup of coffee, watching the sunrise, and thinking that I must have loved Gray once.

When I left him in February, it wasn't because I didn't love him, but because I was afraid if I stayed I'd someday forget that I'd loved him.

Over the eight months and thirt—

It was Friday now. Eight months and fourteen days.

Over the eight months and fourteen days between when I left and now, I had indeed forgotten that I loved him.

Standing here, I realized that *loved him* wasn't accurate.

Love him.

There was no past tense about it.

Maybe I'd been wrong. Maybe I'd been in love with Gray once and lost track of it, but the love itself was still there. I knew that because the thought of losing him was almost a physical pain.

I leaned down and whispered Mark's three other words in his ear. "I love you. Maybe our marriage wasn't working and maybe I wasn't *in love* with you anymore, but I still love you, Gray. Loving you is a part of me."

I stood up straight, picked up my purse and the envelope. "You have to get better."

I gave Alice a small wave and made my way to the lobby of the hospital.

I felt disoriented as I stood looking at the revolving door. That's when I realized that I'd ridden to the hospital in the ambulance with Gray.

I would have to call someone for a ride.

Then I realized my car was still at Steel, Inc. That couldn't be more than a half mile from here. I could walk that, go home, shower, *and* still be back at the hospital in an hour.

I walked through the oversize revolving doors and stepped out into the still-dark morning. The air was brisk, but rather than feeling cold, it felt bracing.

I breathed in a large gulp of it. I hadn't realized how oppressive the pervasive hospital smell was until I breathed in its absence.

I thought about calling JoAnn and Ash as I walked, but I didn't feel up to talking. I sent out a simple text to both of them. *He's stable. Still sedated. I'll text when I know more.*

As I walked, I checked my e-mail, but still nothing from Peggy.

She'd call today, and if she didn't, I'd figure out how to contact her through the cruise line.

I walked down State Street toward Steel, Inc.

A steady wind blew from the north. When the weather got colder, those Canadian winds would blow across the open lake, picking up moisture as it went. When it reached the shore, all that moisture fell to the ground in the form of snow. The process had a name.

Lake effect.

Weather people all along the Great Lakes' shores used the term frequently during the winter. Residents knew the term as well.

Down on Ferncliff, those Canadian winds buffeted the odd collection of fishing shacks. JoAnn's had been renovated sometime in the eighties, years before she bought it. It still retained the look of its fishing-shack roots on the outside, but the inside was from an era of big hair, Pac-Man, and Rubik's Cubes.

Some of the shacks could no longer be called that. They were vacation homes.

The one next to JoAnn's had never been renovated at all. It was the shackiest of them all.

I walked under an overpass, then back into the downtown area. The comedy club and restaurants. No chains here. These were locally owned.

Farther down the street were some shops and banks. The Erie Playhouse was half a block west. For a smaller city, Erie had a vibrant local theater group with wonderful productions. Then the Warner Theater sat in all its glory right on State Street. I loved the great old theater. I had season tickets for the touring Broadway shows that played here.

Walking by the theater and thinking about the shows made me think about what Ash had said. Gray had been listening to Broadway tunes.

I couldn't visualize that. I couldn't imagine him humming or even singing along. Gray wasn't the kind of man who listened to music. He turned on NPR in the car.

Why this sudden fascination with Broadway tunes?

State Street dipped as it came closer to the bay. I could see Steel, Inc. as I stood on the rise. Beyond it, I could see the bay. Beyond that, the peninsula. And though I couldn't see it from here, beyond the peninsula was Lake Erie. Beyond that, London, Ontario.

I could see very far from this vantage point and I could count on what lay beyond what I could see.

Why couldn't I do that for me and Gray?

With him, I couldn't see beyond today. And I couldn't know beyond that.

Once, I believed that I knew exactly how our life would unfold. We'd marry and be deliriously happy . . . ever after.

Ever after wasn't nearly as long as I'd thought it would be.

That was the thought that stuck with me as I walked the rest of the hill to the office. I'd just unlocked my car when Ash pulled into the lot next to my car. "Addie, how is he?"

"I sent you a text," I said.

"*Stable* doesn't say much." His voice and expression were neutral, but I recognized his reproach.

"I'm sorry, Ash. I forget that Gray being sick doesn't affect just me, but you, too."

He nodded, accepting my apology.

"There's really nothing more than that to say," I told him. "Gray's still sedated. They're working on stabilizing his blood pressure. When they feel it'll be safe, they'll take him off the sedation and he'll wake up."

"Then he'll come home?" Ash asked.

I shook my head. "No, it doesn't sound like it. He'll need rehab for a while. And then he'll go home."

Slowly, he asked, "When he comes home will you be there, Addie?"

I didn't need to think about the answer. Maybe I hadn't figured everything out, but this much I knew. "Yes. I'm not going anywhere until he's well."

"But after?" he pressed.

I felt a surge of anger because that was a question I couldn't answer. I remembered that Gray and I had been happy, and I remembered that not only had I once loved him, but I also remembered that I still loved him. But the rest? Could we find our way back to each other? I didn't know.

"Ash, you know I love you, but I'm not going to discuss my marriage with you."

"You need to discuss it with someone," he insisted.

"You're right, I do. With Gray. Not that it will be a discussion. If conversations are ping-pong games, then the ones with Gray are the type where one person bends the table against a wall and plays solo. I hit the ball against a wall, again and again. It bounces back to me without Gray ever touching it. No one can sustain a game like that for long. On their own."

Ash nodded. "A couple of weeks ago I told him he needed to go see you and talk things out. He said he's no good at figuring out what to say. He said he was sure you knew he loved you and there wasn't much to say after that."

"Ash, I do love him, but a relationship should be a dialogue, not a monologue." Maybe that summed it up. Our marriage had been a monologue and, after my straw moment, I simply couldn't sustain it anymore.

I'd been heartbroken and unable to work out what I felt, much less work out what Gray felt. I admitted, "I was lost, Ash. I needed him and he turned away from me."

"That's what I said to him. Obviously, *she doesn't know how you feel this time*."

"What did he say to that?" I asked.

Ash shook his head. "He didn't say anything. He turned around, went into his office, and turned on some music."

That summed up our marriage. When things got difficult, Gray didn't say anything. He just turned away.

I had just officially discussed my problems with my husband more with Ash than Gray and I had ever managed, even with one aborted trip to a therapist.

"I'm running home to grab a shower and change my clothes before I go back," I told Ash.

"Eat something, too, okay?" he said.

I nodded my agreement, if only to stop him from taking me inside and force-feeding me something.

I didn't argue. I simply nodded, closed my car door, and sped away.

A few minutes later I drove down the hill to JoAnn's house on Ferncliff.

I let myself in the door and dropped my purse, anxious to hurry up just in case the hospital tried to call me.

I didn't set the envelope down. I took the papers that I'd carried around for twenty-four hours upstairs. I started to put them on the bed, but instead I found myself walking through the bedroom to the second-story deck. I sat in the chair, opened the envelope, and pulled out the divorce papers.

MARITAL SETTLEMENT AGREEMENT, the header proclaimed in bold, capital letters.

AGREEMENT by and between Adeline Frasier Grayson (hereinafter referred to as "Wife") and Graham R. Grayson, Jr. (hereinafter referred to as "Husband")

I skimmed through all the gobbledygook lawyer-speak.

One sentence stood out.

. . . we now mutually desire to dissolve our marriage and live permanently separate and apart from each other, as if we were single . . .

"As if we were single," I murmured to myself.

I had so much I needed to do, but for the moment, I sat on the deck, looking out at the bay, holding papers that stated I wanted to live my life as if I were single, and I knew it for the lie it was.

What I wanted was Gray.

It's what I'd always wanted.

I remembered our wedding day, just across the bay on Presque Isle peninsula.

❧ ❧ ❧

"Hey, hippie," JoAnn said. "It's time."

"Hippie?" I asked with a laugh. Everything seemed funny today. Everything seemed bright and sparkly.

I'd read stories about prewedding jitters, but I hadn't experienced them. This was where I was meant to be . . . marrying Gray.

I had no family left to speak of and Gray only had his mother. So we decided on a quiet affair—just his mom, our friends, and a district justice whom Gray knew.

I was the one who'd suggested the beach.

Gray agreed, more because it was what I wanted than anything else.

I walked with JoAnn from the tree line across the rocky sand to the water's edge where Gray, his mom, and Ash waited with the district justice. Other friends gathered in a small semicircle.

As I approached, I took Gray's hand and I looked in his eyes. I saw no trace of jitters there either. I simply saw love.

The justice said, "Welcome to this celebration of two people who have come together to join their lives permanently. From this day forth, they'll still be two individuals, but they'll share one heart. Two individuals, but one marriage. Two people with one love."

He nodded at me.

I'd practiced this moment in my mind so many times over the last few weeks. I didn't feel at all nervous as I said, "Gray, I think that I've loved you since the moment I met you in kindergarten. You put your arm around me and said, It's okay. I'm here. *And you've been with me ever since. First as a friend, then as someone I loved. And after today, you'll be something else entirely. You'll be my husband. I promise to love you, care for you, and be with you forever."*

I didn't slip a ring on his finger because Gray wasn't the jewelry kind of guy. But I knew he didn't need a ring to remind him we were married.

The district justice cleared his throat, and Gray said, "I can't be as eloquent as you. Finding the right words has never been my forte, but Addie, I love you. I will always take care of you, and protect you and the family we'll build. I'd give you the world if I could."

He slipped a ring on my finger. He'd wanted to buy something elaborate, but the engagement ring was more than elaborate enough. I'd asked for a simple gold band.

As he slid it on my finger, the justice said, "I now pronounce you husband and wife."

"I love you," I said before he kissed me.

"I love you, too," he replied.

I could almost feel the sand beneath my feet, and hear the waves lap against the breakwalls. I could feel the strength of his embrace and his conviction that he could protect me from anything.

If I could go back, I'd tell him, *"I don't need you to take care of me, I just need you to love me. To hold me. To talk to me."*

I realized there were splotches on the papers I held.

On the heels of that thought, I realized it was my tear. It was quickly joined by others.

I was sobbing. My chest heaved with each one. My nose ran. The crying escalated to the point that I could barely catch a breath between each new wave.

All these months, I hadn't cried. I'd held it together. But Gray being sick was another straw, and it broke my resolve as easily as it had broken the proverbial camel's back. I'd cried yesterday, but this was something else entirely.

I cried for what we'd once been and what we'd lost.

I cried because I might lose him forever.

I'm not sure how long I cried, but suddenly, JoAnn was there, holding me. "Oh, Addie. Is it Gray?"

I nodded. I wanted to tell her he was still alive and stable, but I couldn't force the words out between my sobs.

She didn't ask anything else.

She didn't offer any hollow words. No *I'm sorrys* or *it'll be all rights*.

She simply held me and let me cry.

I cried for Gray. For the life we thought we'd have. For the mess we'd made of everything. I cried for the son I'd wanted with every fiber of my being. The son I'd lost. We'd lost.

Slowly, my sobs subsided.

"He's okay. Gray's okay," I finally said.

JoAnn looked at the papers on my lap. "You don't have to follow through on that."

"I know. But I don't think we can go back. I was remembering our wedding. I was going to love him forever. He was going to take care of me. No matter how many times I told him that I didn't need him to take care of me, I just needed him to stand with me, he didn't get it."

"He never left your side after . . ." She didn't finish the sentence. She didn't need to. That word, *after*, marked a division in my life. There was *before*, and now there was *after*.

Before, I was young and in love. I thought that my love for Gray was enough to see us through anything.

I obviously still hadn't figured out what *after* was.

"Physically, he never left my side. But he left me. I look at him in that bed and I talk to him, like the nurses said. It doesn't feel strange. It feels as if that's been our relationship. Me talking for both of us."

"Addie." She wasn't scolding, or denying the claim. With just my name she was saying she understood. "Tell him again when he wakes up."

I interrupted. "They keep saying he'll have to be careful about his blood pressure. I can't imagine me kicking up a fuss will be good for him."

"It's not a fuss. Needing to be heard isn't necessarily making a scene. Sometimes a whisper is as powerful as a scream," JoAnn said.

I thought about Mark talking about sometimes silence being as good as a prayer.

Sometimes a whisper is as powerful as a scream.

Sometimes silence is as good as a prayer.

Three words matter—"here I am."

The other three words were "I love you."

It felt almost poetic. But poetic or not, I wasn't sure it would help me and Gray. "I don't know if I could take a chance and try to talk it through," I admitted. "I mean, what if . . ."

"Then tell him today," JoAnn said. "Tell him while he's sleeping. Say all the words you need to say."

"What good will it do if he can't hear me?" I asked.

"Maybe it's not just him hearing, maybe it's you saying. Maybe that will help you." JoAnn looked at me, her expression somewhere between sadness and frustration.

I thought about Maude, James with an S, Harriet, Siobhan, Mark, and even Alice. Talking to them had helped a bit. They were strangers who would never know the whole of my story with Gray. But telling them bits, and listening to pieces of their stories had helped me.

I hoped it had helped them, too.

But JoAnn was right, some things I needed to say to Gray. Even if he couldn't hear me, I needed to say them.

"Talk to him," JoAnn said again.

This time I nodded. "I will."

Foolish or not, like Mark had said, there comes a time when the words have to be said.

"And leave the papers here. You shouldn't be carrying them around."

I nodded, knowing she'd think I was agreeing to leave them when actually I was just acknowledging that I shouldn't carry them around, but knowing that I would. Somehow I felt as if I kept ahold of the divorce papers, I could hold on to Gray as well.

It was absurd and I knew it made no sense.

But when I left, I put the now-mangled envelope into my purse and drove back to the hospital.

I'd talked for both of us most of our relationship.

One more time wouldn't hurt.

Chapter Ten

When I walked into the hospital room, I realized that nothing had changed other than Nurse Alice was gone and Gray was in a new position. He was propped facing the tiny window.

"We're trying to avoid pressure ulcers," the dark-haired new nurse said, answering my unasked question.

She had a sunny sort of feel about her. I don't go spouting about auras and the like, but some people just seem to radiate happiness. She was one of those.

"Thank you," I said as I walked back to the chair I spent the night in. I knelt down and studied Gray's face. His color seemed better. There was a pink hue to his cheeks rather than the ghostly white they'd been since his attack. "I'm back, Gray."

"I'm Smita," the new nurse said as if it was nothing out of the ordinary to find a family member talking to a comatose patient. "If you need anything, just ask. I'm only responsible for Mr. Grayson and one other patient today, so I'll be close at hand."

"Thank you," I said. Yesterday I'd said the words countless times by rote, but this time I meant it.

Smita checked the monitors and added, "Alice was right, his vitals are better when you're around."

Her pronouncement brought tears to my eyes. It felt as if my tears were lurking in the background, just looking for any excuse to fall.

"Really, just holler if you need anything," she reiterated as she left the room.

"Thank you again," I called after her.

I sat down in the chair. A patch of sunlight sat squarely on Gray's face. He didn't even squint.

I studied his face. I honestly couldn't remember a time he wasn't a part of my life. I knew that slight scar by his right eyebrow came from a stick that Darryl Smith hit him with. Not that anyone blamed Darryl. Gray was about eight at the time, and they'd been sword fighting.

His face had gone from five o'clock shadow to full-on stubble. Another day or so, he'd have the beginnings of a beard. I ran my fingers across his rough cheek. Gray was the sort of guy who shaved every morning and again in the evening if we were going out.

I'd always preferred him a little scruffy. But right now, I'd give anything if he could get out of this bed and go shave.

Staring at his immobile features hurt. It reminded me how sick he was. I finally had to turn, and looked out the window. From my vantage point, I could see the sky was brightening as the sun started its climb. There were giant puffy fall clouds meandering past the window, so I knew there was a light breeze.

I turned back to Gray, who hadn't moved at all. "It's nice to think everyone is right and my being here helps you," I said. "I feel foolish having a conversation with you while you're unconscious, but I promised Jo."

I didn't know where to start.

I reached into my purse and pulled out the envelope. I didn't set it on the bed, but held it on my lap instead. "I came to your office yesterday to give you these. I know you can't see them, but they're divorce papers. There's a line that says that we are agreeing to live apart from each other, as if we were single."

I looked at that face again . . . I knew it so well. I had planned on looking at it every day for the rest of my life. "Gray, I don't know if I can go back and live as if I'm single, because even when I was single, you were still the biggest part of my life."

I admitted, softly, "I don't know what I want."

I walked to the window again and stared down at the cars. The sun bounced off them, flickering in my eyes. Maybe that explained why I teared up.

Maybe not.

"Since that day in December, everything I thought I knew and could depend on upended. We lost a son, Gray. Do you remember that appointment? You insisted on driving me to all of them. You'd taken me for the blood tests the week before, and that day you were with me when the nurse practitioner started her exam, then got the doctor. I knew something was wrong when he told me he wanted another ultrasound.

"Thinking something might be wrong was so much more difficult than knowing . . ."

Gray drove me to my doctor's appointment. He'd gone to the other two, but this one was special. They were doing a sonogram and said there was a good chance they'd be able to tell the baby's gender.

I'd worn yoga pants and a T-shirt, because I knew they'd make the test easy and I wouldn't have to disrobe.

"I feel like a kid at Christmas," I said as we waited for the tech to come in.

Gray didn't respond. He hadn't said much about the baby. We hadn't planned on starting our family so soon, but sometimes the things we don't see coming end up being all the sweeter. I kept reminding him of that.

"If it's a boy—" I started, but the tech came in and interrupted the game. She had me lie back on the table, then squirted my stomach with gel and started moving the wand around silently.

I waited for her to start pointing out the baby's features, but she worked silently.

"Can you point out what's what?" I finally asked. I reached for Gray's hand and he grabbed mine.

She hesitated a moment, then finally said, "I'm new to this. I'm going to get the doctor and he'll tell you."

She could have given Gray lessons in quietness.

She hurried out of the room and Gray said, "Hunter," in a way that might have seemed random to someone else. But I knew we were picking up the great baby-naming debate. "Timothy," I countered.

He shook his head. "Hunter is a strong name. It—"

The doctor came in, interrupting Gray.

I started to smile, but then saw the doctor's expression. He wasn't my normal doctor but one of his partners. I'd met him on earlier visits. He'd been all smiles and chatty that day, but not now. Not today. His expression told me without words that there would be no joking today.

"I'm just going to have a look," he said.

The doctor's movements were firm and sure as he squirted more of the lubricant on my stomach and then moved the wand until he found what he was looking for.

I didn't watch the screen, but rather watched his face.

His expression told me everything.

I started to cry before he said the words. "I'm sorry. The baby's heart isn't beating."

I gripped Gray's hand. "What?" I asked through my tears.

The doctor wiped the goop from my stomach.

I knew what he'd said. I knew it before he said it. But maybe I was wrong. There had to be some mistake. We were young and healthy. I'd done everything right. I didn't smoke or drink. I'd cut out coffee as soon as I'd found out I was pregnant. I took my prenatal vitamins, drank plenty of water, and did moderate exercise on a daily basis.

"You're wrong. It was beating before," I said. "The baby's in an awkward position, that's all. Tell him, Gray."

But Gray didn't say anything. He continued to hold my hand as I sobbed because I already knew . . .

"Your baby is gone, Mr. and Mrs. Grayson."

The other time I'd seen this physician he'd called me Addie as he measured and checked and we chatted. Now he rested on formality. It gave him distance that I wasn't afforded.

I pulled my hand from Gray's and cradled my stomach.

"He's gone?" I whispered, feeling the weight of the words on my tongue and wishing I hadn't said them. Wishing I could take them back. Wishing the doctor had been called away and had canceled today's appointment.

What I wouldn't give for one more day or hour or minute of ignorance.

One more day of dreams for this child. I'd had so many. Getting into mischief with Harmon and JoAnn's new baby and Wills. Birthday parties. Milestones. First steps. First tooth. First day of school. First dates. First kisses.

"What happens now?" Gray asked as he stood up.

The doctor's expression was still serious, but there was an undercurrent of sympathy as he said, "Mrs. Grayson will have a D and C. It's a procedure that will remove any tissue and . . ."

I reached for Gray's hand again, needing to feel his presence, to feel his support. He wasn't there. He'd taken a couple of steps and stood at the window. His hands were clenched.

He was standing only a foot or so away, but it felt like more.

It felt like so much more.

I cradled my stomach and cried for my child.

How could I love so completely someone I'd never met?

How could someone I loved abandon me so completely at the moment I needed him the most?

ꟸ ꟸ ꟸ

"That moment, when the doctor told us the baby was gone, feels like the first . . ." I didn't know first what. The first moment I pulled away from him? The first moment he'd taken a step away from me?

"We'd been so happy on the way to that appointment. We were still arguing about names. I wanted to name him Timothy and you wanted to name him Hunter. After we left, there was no reason to argue about names. There was no reason to argue at all. We couldn't do anything for our son. He was dead. My hand rested on my stomach and I realized I'd never feel him kick. He'd never . . ."

I started to cry now, though I hadn't cried then.

I cried for all the things our son would never do. All the dreams I'd had for him that were dashed in that one moment.

He'd never take a breath.

He'd never learn to crawl or say *Mama.*

He'd never start school, fall in love, have his heart broken, then fall in love again.

He'd never get married and have children.

All my dreams for this baby died in that examining room.

And after that first moment I hadn't cried for him. After the shock, I'd gone numb.

Gray didn't cry either.

He'd never said he was suffering, too.

We didn't talk about the baby. We didn't talk . . . period.

The next day he drove me to the hospital . . .

The nurse started an IV in my hand. "This will all be over soon," she said. "You're lucky you weren't further along. We'll give you something that will relax you. They'll put you to sleep and before you know it, the procedure will be over and you can get back to your life."

She left the room. And I lay there, an IV in my hand, wondering how she expected me to simply go back to my life. As if I'd never been pregnant. As if I didn't have a room full of baby furniture, still boxed up. Still waiting to be put together for this baby.

This baby who would never be.

I wiped a hand across my cheeks. I was shocked that there were no tears there.

Gray stood next to me. His hands were clasped behind his back and his spine was ramrod straight.

The baby would never throw his arms around me and hug me. He'd never kiss me.

He'd never tell me he loved me or hear me say the words to him.

And then I realized my sorrow was for me as well. For the mother I wouldn't have a chance to be.

I wanted to be the mother who rocked him to sleep, who thought everything he did was wonderful, who sang him lullabies. I'd never be the mother who read him stories and chased monsters from under his bed.

I thought about Gray and the father he never got to grow into. He hadn't planned it and wasn't good at navigating without a road map. But I knew in my heart he'd have loved our son. He would have grown into a wonderful father.

He might not have had a father as a role model, but he had his mom, and Peggy was one of the best parents I'd ever met.

I tried to say good-bye to the child I'd never know. I tried to say good-bye to all my dreams and hopes for him.

"We lost our baby," I said.

"Maybe it's for the best . . ." Gray started, but he let the sentence die there. Probably because of my look of horror.

The tears I couldn't shed dried up at the moment.

They wheeled me down to the room where the doctor said something about removing the product of conception.

I wanted to scream, this wasn't a product of conception. It was a baby.

My baby.

"We'd had that blood test the week before . . . everything happened. When the lab called with the results, not knowing we'd lost the baby, they said there were no genetic anomalies. There was nothing wrong with our baby. The lab didn't know about the D and C. And when I asked about the gender, the tech said he was a boy."

My hand rested on my stomach. For just a few short months, it had sheltered our baby . . . our son.

I hadn't cried for him.

And after that moment, I didn't reach for Gray again, either. Every time I did, I could hear the words *Maybe it's for the best . . .*

"After I lost the baby—" I faltered.

I didn't want to do this. How could saying the words to Gray help? It wouldn't change anything.

I remembered my promise to JoAnn and pushed the words past the lump in my throat. "So many people said unthinking things. I knew even as they said them that they didn't mean to be cruel. They'd tell me that we were young. We could have another baby. I wanted to scream, *but we'd never have this baby.* I think that maybe even worse were the people who ignored the fact I'd been pregnant altogether. As if the baby we'd lost had never existed."

I looked at Gray. I no longer saw the wires and tubes, I saw him. And I saw him in so many happier memories. But I also saw the one moment that had become the wedge that broke us apart.

"When I woke up after the D and C, I reached for you, but you held yourself apart. You had said, *Maybe. It's. For. The. Best.*"

The words didn't slip out; I pushed them. One by one.

"Maybe it was for the best for you. We could go back to your precious timetable and have a baby at the correct, appointed time. But we'd never have *this* baby. Our son. Losing him? It wasn't for the best. After that, you didn't say anything."

Nothing.

"That moment—those words—it feels like I've been stuck there ever since. We didn't talk about the baby. You shut the door to the nursery when we got home and we walked by it every day, but we didn't open it.

"And every one of those moments piled on that first one until those moments were all I could feel and remember."

For months, all I could hear was Gray saying maybe my worst moment was for the best.

I tried. We went to counseling. I planned a honeymoon.

But try as I might, I couldn't get beyond that moment or those words.

"How did I lose you? You were the one constant in my life. How did I let you go? How did you let me go? Everything from before disappeared in that one moment, and I couldn't find my way back to you. I couldn't find my way back to the way we used to be."

And the tears I'd denied myself for eight months now flowed freely.

"How did we lose each other?" That was the question I kept asking.

"Yesterday," I told him, "when you were in surgery and I waited for you, other moments squeezed past that awful place I'd been stuck. I remembered our first dance, I remembered the night you showed me the house and asked me to marry you. I remembered our wedding, Gray."

I could almost hear JoAnn saying, *Hey, hippie, it's time.* I could almost feel the sand in my toes and see Gray waiting for me.

"When Maude asked about our first date, I couldn't tell her. It's not that it was anything huge. In the scope of first dates it was probably fairly middle of the road. But I remember it, and, to me, that date changed everything. You'd always been my friend, and sometimes I used to wish you'd see me as more.

"Then that night. It didn't even start as a date. We were just two friends going out and . . ."

I unzipped my coat as we walked toward the seating area of the Cornerstone Bar and Grill. "I'm not sure I'll get too many more sunsets this season."

I didn't take the coat off because I was still half numb.

Late fall in Erie could be colder than some places' winters. Blue skies became rarer as autumn began to deepen into winter. Even my layers weren't enough to make tonight's sunset a comfortable one.

Despite the cold, I was glad we'd both stayed in Erie for college.

"Pretty soon we'll have to watch the sun set beyond ice dunes," I said.

I crawled into the booth, and instead of sitting on the other side like he normally would, Gray slid in next to me.

"Is there something wrong with that side?" I asked, laughing.

"The Steelers are playing," he said, nodding toward the television that hung on the far wall. I did not follow sports, but I knew he did, and being able to see a game was enough of a justification for just about anything.

"Want me to move over there?" I asked. Even though I'd scooted over in the booth as far as I could, Gray's thigh was still brushing against mine.

His expression didn't change, but I saw teasing in his eyes. "I'm not afraid of your cooties."

I laughed. "I haven't thought about cooties for years. They were all the rage in second grade. Ms. Timmons gave a lecture that day about how there was no such thing as a cootie, but all us girls knew that all you boys had them. Some more than others."

He nodded, then turned his attention back to the game.

"Paul Humphreys asked me out," I said. Paul had sort of attached himself to me in our Bio I class. We were lab partners now. Yes, he was okay, but my feelings for him were lackluster at best. "I'm not sure if I want to, though. I guess he's nice enough, but I don't know."

Maybe that was enough of a reason not to. Nice enough *wasn't a good enough reason to date someone.*

The waitress came and I ordered our usual pizza with everything except anchovies.

"Don't," Gray said, quietly, his eyes still on the game.

"Don't what?" I asked. I thought maybe he was talking to the players, though Gray wasn't one of those animated fans who talked back to sportscasters and audibly cheered their team. He didn't wave a Terrible Towel, or holler at the refs.

"Don't go out with Paul," Gray said simply.

"Why not? He's nice enough and he—"

I didn't get any further because Gray turned away from the television and his game . . . and kissed me. Not just some peck on the cheek. Not even some quick kiss. This was a kiss that spoke of a hunger I had very little experience with. It was a hunger that I wasn't equipped to deal with in my teens.

It spoke of something more than the friendship I'd always thought we had.

Gray ended the kiss and sat back in his original position.

"That's why" was all he said. He went back to watching the game, but he draped his arm over my shoulder.

It felt right there.

"Gray, should we talk about this?" I asked. He'd been my friend all through school. And there were a few times I thought that maybe we could

be something more, but those moments of possibility always passed before either of us acted on them.

"Do you need to talk about this?" he countered.

"Probably," I admitted.

He'd all but forgotten the game and didn't even glance toward the screen when the rest of the restaurant cheered. He gave me his total focus as he said, "Okay, shoot."

"So was that kiss your way of saying we're dating?" I asked.

"I think that maybe we've been dating for months, only neither of us realized it. Something has changed."

I had noticed that since we'd started college and our classes didn't intersect, Gray had made an effort to get together with me a few times a week. "I thought we were just friends hanging out."

"Can we be both?" he asked.

Slowly, I nodded. "Sure we can . . ."

"I guess the question is, do you want to?" He took his arm from my shoulder and looked at me, waiting.

"Gray, you've been my friend since that first day of school. You know me better than anyone else. Moving from friendship to . . . well, something more, makes sense."

"Making sense doesn't mean that's what you want," he pointed out in that very logical way of his. Sometimes that logic drove me crazy, and sometimes it was what I loved about him.

I loved that he charted a course and stuck to it.

I had no clue what I wanted. I was an art major mainly by default. I had no idea what I'd do with the degree. Gray knew he wanted to go into business.

His sense of direction was a nice foil to my lack of it.

So many things about him seemed to fill in the things I was lacking.

He was quiet . . . I wasn't.

He was steady . . . I could be a bit of a will-o'-the-wisp.

He guarded his emotions . . . I wore mine on my sleeve.

I'd never thought about it, but maybe he filled in the pieces I was missing, and maybe I filled in things for him that he was missing.

Maybe it wasn't the ways we were alike that made us work as friends; maybe it was the ways we weren't alike that made our friendship work.

And maybe those things would work all the better if we moved beyond friendship into some new territory.

*"It is what I want, though," I told him. I realized there was no doubt, no worries, just a sense of certainty. Gray was exactly who and what I wanted. "*More *is what I want."*

"Okay, then." He put his arm back over my shoulders, leaned back, and watched the game.

He was smiling.

"I want to go slow," I said.

Without looking from the screen he said, "Addie, we've been moving toward this since kindergarten. I think I can handle slow."

I started to laugh and he tightened his arm around me.

The waitress came with our sodas. Both had one of those plastic drink animals. Swans. They hung from the glass by their necks.

We'd eaten at the Cornerstone many times, but had never had animals on our drinks. "Are they new?" I asked her.

She shook her head. "The bartender puts them on mixed drinks. We have a bucket of them. I pulled these out for you two because . . ." She stopped and looked a little embarrassed, as if thinking better of the plastic swans.

"Because?" I pressed.

She chuckled in a way that it was apparent she was laughing at herself. "Because you look so cute, snuggled together on the bench. I had to hunt to find the swans. We have a lot more giraffes and monkeys than swans."

"Why swans?" I asked. Gray was intent on watching the game and seemingly ignoring us.

"Call me a romantic—Chuck the bartender does—but I always try to find them for the couples that have . . . well, something special."

She blushed, and looked as if she'd suck the words back in if she could.

Before either of us could ask what that meant, she said, "I'll be back with your pizza in a few minutes."

"I don't remember who won the game," I said. "But I do remember when we finished, you picked up your swan and tucked it in your pocket. I kept mine as well."

I looked at him and I felt the tears start down my cheek. "When you collapsed, I saw that picture of us and the swan. I grabbed them. They're right here on your nightstand. And I remembered, Gray. After months of not being able to move past that one bad moment, I've remembered so many of the others."

I'd done nothing but remember since we came to the hospital.

"I remember that I loved you then. And thinking I could lose you made me realize that I still love you. I don't know if I can get past all those other moments since December. They're still there and they still hurt. But when I read the words in the divorce decree, *as if we were single,* I knew no matter what, I'd never be able to live as if I hadn't been married to you. And I'd never not love you. I think part of the problem is that after we lost the baby, I forgot to fill in your missing spaces. My heart was gaping and bleeding, and I was so busy trying to stem the flow, I just forgot. You were ready to just move on without a backward glance. But I couldn't. And maybe I couldn't forgive you for being able to just get over it so easily."

I sighed. "I guess what I'm saying is, I'm here. I'm all-in. When you're better we'll see where we stand. But no matter what, I won't forget all our good moments again, and I'll try to move past losing the baby. I wanted—no, I needed—to grieve with you, but you didn't grieve."

"That's not so." I jumped at the sound of someone's voice.

Chapter Eleven

I knew that voice.

I turned and saw Peggy in the doorway.

"Gray, your mother's here," I said before I rushed to her and hugged her for all I was worth. "You're here. I hadn't heard from you and I'd started to get worried. I was going to try to contact you on the ship today."

She hugged me back. "Oh, honey, I'm so sorry. I should have sent a reply. I got your e-mail and I just spun into action. It feels like I've been spinning since I read it. I got off the boat on the island and I've been making my way here since."

Peggy's dark hair was laced with gray and caught up in a messy bun. She was wearing a sundress and sandals, despite the fact it was October. The thin cardigan that would be perfect in the tropics looked woefully inadequate for Erie.

"I thought you'd have to finish the cruise," I said.

"As if they could make me." Peggy looked formidable as she snorted, and I realized that I wouldn't have wanted to be the person who tried to keep her on the cruise ship after she'd read my e-mail.

She shook her head. "They tried to tell me that it would be faster to just take the cruise ship home, but I got off and found a private pilot who flew me back to Florida, and from there, I found a flight home. Even if the cruise had been faster, I wouldn't have been able to sit there, relaxing, knowing he was here, sick, and you were on your own."

I felt slightly envious of her. I'd been doing just that . . . sitting here. Inactive. Inert. Waiting.

She'd been working to get here. She'd had a purpose.

I hugged her. "I'm so glad you're here."

Ours had never been one of those stereotypical in-law relationships. I loved Peggy. Next to JoAnn, I was closer to her than anyone . . . anyone other than Gray, once upon a time.

"I spent Gray's money," she added, a bit shamefaced.

"It wasn't Gray's, it was yours. He put that money aside for a house for you," I said. I knew how much he wanted to show his mom how thankful he was. When he'd found a house and wanted to buy it for her as a gift, I'd understood. Granted, buying someone a house was over the top, but the thought—the feeling—behind it was so sweet. "When you wouldn't let him buy the house, he set up that account. It was his way of paying you back for helping him get through college—"

"I didn't pay his tuition," she protested.

"You helped him make up the difference, and you kept a roof over his head," I said, parroting his arguments in the past. "I don't think this was how he intended you use it, but it was yours to do as you please."

"He is so stubborn he wouldn't take it back, but I've held on to it for him. But I just had to be here. I'm his mother," she said as if that statement explained everything. And in a way it did.

"Come on," I said, bringing her farther into the room. We walked around the bed to the side he was facing. I explained all I knew and then added, "The doctors are keeping him in a coma until they feel he's out of the woods."

Peggy walked up to Gray, and I heard her sharp intake of breath as she really saw him.

I'd already grown accustomed to the tubes and wires. I just saw *him* now when I looked at him. But I remembered my shock when they'd brought me in yesterday.

She ran her finger across his stubbled cheek, before leaning down and kissing his forehead. "I'm here, honey," she said.

I thought about Mark. Maybe he was right. Sometimes *here I am* was enough.

"Thank you, Peggy," I said, for both me and for Gray.

"I'm sorry I left you on your own for so long," she said to me.

"I knew you'd be here as soon as you could. He's doing better," I said.

"You don't look like you're doing better. Frankly, you look like hell," Peggy said in her shoot-from-the-hip way. She smiled to soften the words, but I knew she was right. If I looked anything like I felt, her description was generous.

She said, "I heard what you were saying when I came in."

"I'm sorry." I wasn't sure why I was apologizing. "There was so much I wanted to tell him. So much I should have said months ago."

"So much *he* should have said months ago," she said gently. "I love my son, but that boy could give a monk a run for his money."

I laughed and hiccuped as it became almost a sob.

"So tell me everything," Peggy said.

I did. It was as if talking to strangers in the hospital had suddenly made talking to someone I loved easier. I told her all of it.

Except for the divorce papers. Those I kept to myself.

I thought she'd tell me that I needed to give him another chance. That the two of us could make it through this.

I realized I desperately wanted her to say those things.

Maybe if she believed we could make it through this, I could as well.

Instead she simply asked, "Have you heard when they're going to wake him up?"

"No. I was hoping the doctor would give us some idea today."

Peggy nodded then leaned down and whispered into his ear. She placed her hand on his fingertips, much like I had earlier.

We both stood next to him. I watched as his chest rose and fell to the rhythm of the machine that was pumping air into his lungs. Then I turned slightly and watched the liquid in the bag drip one slow drop at a time, into the line that snaked down to the hand Peggy was holding.

Peggy had gotten a manicure, I noticed. The fact might not have stood out so much on someone else, but Peggy was a waitress. Her nails, while nicely trimmed, were normally polish-free. She'd once joked they were working hands.

At the moment, they were hands that were giving comfort. I saw them tighten against Gray's fingertips as she said, "You're wrong, you know."

I couldn't remember what we'd been talking about and had no idea what she was referring to. "About?"

"About the baby," she said softly, as if hearing her mention it would upset me.

No one talked about the baby—not even me. I realized how much I craved hearing him mentioned. Maybe I needed to know that even though he had never drawn a breath, he had mattered to someone other than me. That someone else mourned his loss.

"Addie, I haven't seen my son cry since he was little. He didn't cry when his father left. He's stoic. But after the doctor told you there was no hope, he took you home, got you to sleep, and came to see me. Addie, I've never seen anyone so broken up."

"He never—" Never. He'd never cried. He'd never seemed upset.

Maybe. It's. For. The. Best. Those words were the cornerstone of the wall that had grown up between us.

"He cried, Addie. He didn't say much, but he cried. For you. For the baby. Maybe for himself."

"He never said anything to me," I said again. "I never saw him shed a tear."

"That's my fault, you know," Peggy said. "Just like him being in the hospital is my fault." She didn't cry. Like Gray, she wasn't a woman to wear her emotions on her sleeve. While Gray might have a serious default expression, Peggy wore a perpetual smile.

Someone who didn't know her might not notice that there were times that smile didn't reach her eyes.

She offered me a small one now. "It is my fault. After his father left, Gray felt he had to take care of me. I tried to tell him I didn't need him to take care of me, but he never listened. It got worse as he got older. Like when he tried to buy me a house. It was his way of saying he loved me. And when I wouldn't take his house, the money he put in the bank for me . . . that was the same thing. He can't put his feelings into words, but he tries to show them."

"Peggy, Gray's condition isn't anyone's fault." I tried to reassure her, but it was hard since I felt guilty as well. I knew he didn't know why I'd come to his office, but knowing and feeling . . . those were two very different things.

Peggy shook her head, not believing me. "Honey, how much did he ever tell you about his father?"

"Not much. He said his father left when he was seven and he hadn't seen him since. He didn't want to see him."

Peggy nodded. "Graham—Gray's father—was a screwup. He couldn't hold a job, couldn't manage much of anything. Even then I was waitressing and my income supported the family. The good thing was, I had someone to leave Gray with whenever Graham got laid off or fired from another job. And then one day, I got a call from a cop. Gray had been found downtown with no adult. The officer was concerned."

"How old was he?" How had he never told me this?

"Seven. That's when his father left. I kicked Graham out that night and told him not to come back until he was ready to be a parent. It wasn't so much the work, or lack thereof, but how could I be with a man I couldn't trust with our son? *My* son. Graham, even at his best, had never been a very invested parent. What would have happened if Gray had wandered into the wrong place, or been picked up by the wrong person? In my opinion, that cop saved my son's life."

"Did his dad ever contact him?" I asked.

Peggy shook her head. "We never heard from him again. The last time Gray ever spoke to me about his father was the day after Graham left. We'd called Gray *Little Graham* before his dad left. Sometimes *LG*. The day after his dad left, he told me to call him Gray."

"He was seven?" I tried to remember a time when Gray was Graham. We'd gone to school together, so those first couple of years he must have been Graham, but in my mind he was Gray. He'd always been Gray.

My mind had rewritten that part of his past. My past.

How often do our minds rewrite our memories?

Had my mind rewritten other memories?

After we lost our son, I was so sure that Gray was aloof, but had he thought he was being strong? Being strong in order to take care of me? I'd been so angry after we lost the baby. Had that anger tinted my perception, or my memories?

Peggy shook her head. "We never heard from Gray's father again. A friend told me that Graham ended up in Michigan, but he never sent Gray as much as a birthday card."

Or a child-support check.

Gray had said that much when he'd wanted to buy his mom a house. He'd wanted to make up for her having to be his sole support when he was a kid.

"I'm sorry," I said.

"Don't be. I'd fallen out of love with Graham a long time before that. I'd stayed with him for Gray. When I saw that he wasn't there for his son, asking him to leave was the easiest thing I'd ever done. Easy on me, but not so easy on Gray."

"Peggy, he might not have talked about it, and I'm sure he missed his dad, or at least missed the idea of one. But that, and this"—I waved at the machine next to Gray's bed—"aren't your fault. And not having his dad around certainly didn't make him sick."

"Don't you see? Wandering away that day was the last truly childish thing he ever did. He was only seven. He got straight As in school. He worked his way through college and only let me help a few terms when he simply couldn't pay the tuition on his own."

Her guilt over Gray's abbreviated childhood was evident on her face. I reached for her, but she shook her head.

"Peggy . . ." I started, but didn't know what words would comfort her.

"He tried to give me a house, Addie," she said. "I mean, *a house*. He said that all he ever wanted to do was take care of me. I gave it so much thought on the way here, and I think he wanted to make up for his dad leaving. I think that's why he worked so hard. And that's why he's here."

"Peggy, you didn't make him—" I started.

She cut me off. "We always had enough, but never anything extra when he was growing up. He worked so hard to put himself through college. He's stood on his own two feet. Even though he has you and me, he's stood on his own."

"Gray loves his work. That's not on you . . ." I started to abdicate blame for myself as well, but I wasn't as sure about that.

Peggy caught the hesitation. "Or you?"

"Or me," I told her, though I wasn't quite sure that's how I felt. I felt guilty.

But as for him loving work? After the baby, I'd minded. I'd felt he was hiding behind his work.

But I suddenly remembered that there was a time I hadn't minded.

"He canceled another honeymoon because of work?" Peggy asked, shaking her head. "Are you furious?"

I laughed. "No. He was right. They have some big negotiations going on at work, and Jo and I are taking a trip in a few weeks to meet some more carpenters out of Lancaster. It's not a good time."

"At the rate he's going, you'll never go on a honeymoon."

"Don't tell him, but it's okay," I stage-whispered. "He'll take me to the beach and we'll watch a sunset and that'll be enough. Especially if we stop for ice cream after."

Peggy snorted, but she smiled.

"There are two things that Gray's passionate about, family and work. And on any given day it's a toss-up which is on top." I laughed.

Peggy did too.

"You're wrong," Gray said as he walked into the living room. "Family will always be first. Business is just a way to take care of my family."

"A way you love," I said, still teasing, waiting to see that long, slow smile soften his expression.

Still serious, he said, "Yes, but not as much as I love you two."

"I guess we'll have to forgive him for being late for dinner," I said to Peggy. "I mean, that was too sweet."

"And the honeymoon?" Peggy asked, giving Gray a mom look.

"Yeah. Like I said, he can owe me a sunset," I quipped.

"And ice cream," Gray added, finally smiling.

"And ice cream. And I'm not talking about being a cheap date here. I'm talking about a large ice cream. With sprinkles."

"He loves his work. It's not our fault and it's not work's fault. This condition is rare to begin with, and when it does occur it's normally in men much older than Gray. There could be a genetic component, or there could have been some underlying anomaly. They may do more tests as he recovers, but there's a good chance we'll never know exactly why this happened. But he can recover and he can live a normal life with medication. He'll go back to the work he loves. He'll just have to make some lifestyle changes."

"And will you be a part of that normal life?" she asked.

I nodded. I would be there at least until we saw where we stood.

"He was devastated when you lost the baby," she said again, as if to be sure I believed her.

It should have helped, knowing that he mourned the baby as well. But knowing that made me feel worse.

Gray had seen how I was suffering and let me think I was alone in my grief. Rather than face our darkest moment together, he let us both face it on our own.

I nodded, but I wasn't sure I believed her.

"He's always felt as if he had to be responsible for me," she said again. "I don't know that I'd realized how much until he tried to buy me that house."

I remembered the day two years ago. Gray had come home, so excited that the small house at the end of the block was for sale.

I have a plan, he'd said . . .

"I have a plan. I'm going to buy my mom a house," Gray said as he walked into the house one day after work.

The comment came from out of nowhere and I wasn't sure how to respond, so I simply said, "Okay."

"She's spent her whole life working, trying to take care of me on her own after my father left. Before he left, if I'm honest. I started putting money into an account for her as soon as the business started turning a profit. That small Cape down the block has a For Sale *sign in the yard. It would be perfect. She'd be close, but not too close. I want to buy it and surprise her. And—"*

"Gray," I said, stopping his list of reasons in its tracks. Gray, who wasn't loquacious on his best day, rattled off all those words as if he were reading from cue cards. "Gray, I know you've always set money aside for your mom, but even if you hadn't, I'd say yes. But with one caveat. No surprising her. Maybe Peggy doesn't want to move."

"Why wouldn't she? I worry about her in that house all by herself."

"I know. But, Gray, you said it yourself, she worked so hard to support you both. She certainly deserves the life she wants now. Maybe it will mean living down the block, or maybe for her, it means living where she's at now. Or maybe something else entirely. So talk to her first."

❧❧❧

Peggy shook her head. "He was so confused when I said no. I mean, genuinely befuddled by the idea I might not want him to take care of me. I was almost insulted when he took all that money he'd saved and put it in that account for me. But when I was trying to get home, it was a godsend."

"I'm glad it helped get you home," I said.

"I'll never be rich, but I love what I do, and I'm proud of what I've accomplished," Peggy said.

"I don't think he meant to minimize that," I said, defending Gray.

"No," she said. "I'm sure he didn't."

"Being strong and taking care of us. I think that's one way Gray tells us he loves us without words." As I said the words, I realized that maybe that's what he was trying to do for me after we lost our son.

Maybe he didn't see himself as being distant. Maybe he thought he was being strong for me. Supporting me.

I remembered him waiting on me the first few days I was home, then afterward, he was always nagging me to get out of the house, go for a walk, go see a sunset, all the things I used to love that had lost their appeal.

"I didn't need a cheerleader," I said softly. "I didn't even need a shoulder. I needed someone who understood what I was going through because he was going through the same thing."

"Maybe Gray didn't know that. My son is sometimes a bit obtuse about things like that."

I snorted. "More than a bit."

"He always had you to remind him. Like not buying me a house as a surprise. I don't think he knew what to do when you stopped reminding him of things. You two have been joined at the hip since you started school. He can't function properly without you."

Peggy and I stood next to each other, her hand still positioned over his fingers.

I looked down at Gray, and the now-familiar noise of the machines was the only sound. I realized that I had stopped trying.

When I'd tried to force that trip to St. Lucia, it was very much the same thing as when he'd wanted to buy his mom a house. I was trying to back him into the corner and force him to do what I wanted. To be what I wanted him to be.

I thought that maybe getting away after we lost the baby would somehow help us reconnect. Maybe even find our way back to where we were before the tragedy.

But I'd never said those words to Gray. I'd never explained why I'd planned a trip for us. I'd simply handed him the itinerary, and when he'd said he wasn't sure he could make it work, I'd walked away.

Smita came in and checked the machines, noting the figures on Gray's chart.

"Peggy, this is Gray's nurse today. Smita, this is Gray's mom, Peggy."

"Hi, Mrs. Grayson." She paused a moment and eyed both of us. "Technically, he should only have one visitor at a time. I don't mind if you both are here, but he'll be in the hospital for a while. It might be better to take turns."

She paused again then added, "And I don't want to be the bearer of bad news, but you both look like hell. Neither of you will do Mr. Grayson any good if you don't take care of yourselves."

She turned and left the room.

I looked at Peggy and knew that Smita's observation was right . . . her trip home had cost her. I could try to send her for some rest, but I knew how much she needed to be with him.

"Why don't you take some time with him?" I offered. "I'll go home, catch a nap, and then come back, and you can head home and get some sleep, too."

"Are you sure?" Peggy asked.

"He needs us. Both of us. Smita's right, we won't do him any good if we make ourselves sick." I hugged Peggy and took one last look at Gray. "If there's any change, or if the doctor comes down, call me?"

"I will," she promised. "Thank you, Addie."

"If you get tired and want to head home before I get here, just call." I kissed Gray on the forehead. "I'll be back soon."

I remember thinking that the hospital's corridors were like a maze when I first came here, but I navigated to the elevators with no problem. I'd come to think of them as the hub. I just had to remember how to get back to them in order to get around.

Maybe if I could figure out my hub with Gray, I could get back to us.

I thought about heading to Ferncliff, but I hated that the reception there was so inconsistent.

I found myself driving home instead.

Maybe that word explained why.

The house on Ferncliff was where I lived. The house on Willow Lane was *home*.

Chapter Twelve

I pulled up in front of our Willow Lane home. I could almost see the two of us on that first visit so long ago.

I stood at the gate.

The metal was cold in my hand.

The squeak that had once been a soft sound had deepened and turned gravelly in the months since I'd last been here.

I stood for a moment, ghost images of that first visit playing through my mind. Gray and I had been so happy.

We'd had so many plans.

I walked through the gate.

The plants in the front of the house were all dying off in the cool fall nights. Normally, I'd have planted mums, simply to keep color in the garden just a little longer.

Gray hadn't done that.

The ivy that framed the door was in the process of dying back as well. There were still spots of dull green, but most of the leaves were turning brown.

I walked up to the arched door and held my keychain in my hand. I fumbled through the keys, looking for the one for the house.

I'd never taken it off my key ring. I'd simply added a key to the Ferncliff house. I didn't need labels to know what each key was for. Harbor House, Ferncliff, my car. Gray's car. Willow Lane.

The key felt foreign as I plucked it from the rest and slipped it into the lock.

I opened the door for the first time in months and stepped inside the house, shutting the door behind me.

I dropped the keys into the bowl on the small hall table. I hung my purse from the hook I'd always used. I took my phone out and put it in my back pocket, in case the hospital or Peggy called.

I started to set the envelope down as well, but in the end, I carried it with me.

I stepped into the living room. It looked the same as it always had. Even the throw pillows on the couch were propped the way I'd have done them.

I stopped in front of the fireplace. The Helen Allingham print I'd bought for the house hung where it always had. Pastoral. Homey. That's what I'd tried to achieve here in the house . . . a home.

There were logs in the fireplace so that it would only take a match to get a fire going. For a moment, I was tempted. I remembered our first night here, on an air mattress in front of the fire. I remembered thinking I could have been content to always stay like that.

But we couldn't.

And here we were.

I picked up a match, ready to light the fire, but I set it back down. I wouldn't want to leave a fire burning if I had to run back to the hospital.

The large buffet in the dining room shone, as if it had been recently polished.

The kitchen was the same as the other rooms, cleaned and in the same sort of order I'd have kept it.

I opened the refrigerator. Other than the water pitcher and a quart of milk, it was barren. The pantry was pretty sparsely filled as well.

What had Gray been eating in the months since I left?

I knew that his condition wasn't brought about by a bad diet, but I had to think that being run-down wouldn't help his recovery.

I thought about opening the freezer. Gray had said he'd bought ice cream for when I was home. Well, I was here. I could open it up and eat some. But I found I couldn't face it.

Part of me wanted to go curl up and nap on the couch, but instead, I turned to the stairs. I walked up them slowly and hesitated on the landing. All the doors were shut.

Rather than go to our bedroom, I turned to the door to the left of the stairs. My hand hesitated on the doorknob. Part of me didn't want to open it, but I knew I had to.

Everything was exactly the same here as well. The box with the crib was in the corner. A plastic package of soft flannel sheets with monkeys on them on top. I'd opened the box for the mobile with black-and-white circles when I brought all the items up.

I wound the music box part of it now and the tinkling rendition of "Brahms' Lullaby" filled the room.

Bags of baby clothes. I remembered how fascinated I'd been by how small they were.

There was a bookshelf under the window next to the recliner. When I'd found out I was pregnant, I'd gone on a book-buying splurge on Amazon. All my childhood favorites were stacked on the shelves, waiting to read to the baby.

I ran my fingers along the shelf, surprised that there didn't seem to be any dust on it. It had been months since I left. Months since the day Gray had shut the door to this room.

And yet the room had obviously been cleaned, the same as the rest of the house.

I sat in the recliner, pushed the footrest up, and covered up with the soft, cream-colored throw that I'd placed on the back of it.

The throw smelled of Gray.

I curled up around it, drinking in the scent of him.

In my mind's eye, I could suddenly picture Gray coming home to the empty house and making his way to this half-formed room. He'd kick off his shoes, cover up with this blanket in this chair, and . . .

Did he cry for our son?

Did he mourn for the child who never stood a chance?

From under the blanket, I stared at the room. I remembered the day he'd painted it. He'd used low-VOC paint, but still insisted I couldn't spend the weekend in the house.

It was the week before that last trip to the doctor's.

Ten months ago.

That weekend was the last time I remembered being truly happy . . .

". . . it's so hard to spend much time down here because Wills is so small," JoAnn said after she'd tucked Wills into the portable crib in the master bedroom and come back into the second room where I was staying. "I keep imagining that he is eying the balcony, thinking he could rappel from it. Harmon's been talking about renting it out for a few years, until the kids are older. I asked if he wanted to sell it, but he said he might want a boat someday."

"Harmon in a boat?" Harmon was a wonderful man, but he felt like someone who would be more at home in an ivy-encased library than on a

boat. JoAnn laughed as she nodded. "Not just any boat, a sailboat. He wants to teach Wills and the new baby to sail."

"I didn't know he sailed."

"He doesn't."

She laughed and I joined in. Her husband was a sweetheart, but Harmon was not what I pictured when I thought sailor. He was more of a man who after a day in a library would head to an Irish pub. I could picture him with a Guinness in hand, singing along with some folk tune.

I realized it was easy to picture because we'd all gone out and he'd done just that more than once.

"Well, if Harmon says he wants to learn to sail so he can teach the kids, he will. That husband of yours is the most determined man I've ever met. He saw you, fell for you, and decided to win your heart, and he did. And you weren't easy, my friend."

JoAnn laughed. "Harmon was not the type of man I normally dated."

I snorted. "You can say that again. The men you normally dated were losers. Harmon is not that."

"No, he's not," she agreed. "I think we both got lucky with our husbands."

"I do, too," I admitted. "But then again, they were even luckier."

JoAnn laughed. "They were. Are."

I nodded.

She glanced at her watch. "We should probably call it a night. I need to get some sleep or I'll never be able to function tomorrow."

"Me, too." I got up. "Night."

JoAnn started toward the door then stopped, her hand on her stomach, which was definitely rounded. I put mine on my still-flat stomach and realized I couldn't wait to see the evidence of my baby. I could imagine my stomach swelling as our baby grew.

My baby and JoAnn's would grow up together. Hopefully, they'd be friends.

We were thrilled that we'd have children who would be so close in age.

"You remember when we were younger and would have spent a girls' weekend partying all night?" she asked. "When did we get so old?"

I rested my hand on my stomach. "When we started having kids. Peggy assures me if this baby's anything like Gray I may not sleep for a couple of years after he's born. And if your new one is anything like Wills . . ."

"We both better get some sleep now, then," JoAnn said with a laugh.

She went next door to the master bedroom. I heard the door shut.

I went out to the second-story deck. It could be accessed from either of the bedrooms. I was careful to stay at my end and not disturb JoAnn and Wills.

I sat out on one of the lounge chairs. This was a view I didn't think I'd ever get tired of. Ferncliff sat on the city side of the bay and looked out to Presque Isle, the peninsula that made up the other side of the bay.

The beaches were closed at sundown, but there were a few lights visible. Maybe they were rangers? Maybe they were lights on buildings? Whatever they were, they were enough to make the peninsula have some sense of form even in the dark of a moonlit night.

But what I loved the most out here was the night sky.

The stars seemed so much brighter, so much closer.

I wished my phone had some bars down here. I would have liked to call Gray and say good night. I'd love to sit here on the deck, watching the stars and knowing he was just a phone call away.

"Addie," someone called in a stage whisper. "Look down."

I got up and looked down beneath the deck to the bit of walkway between the house and the bay. "I feel like I should quote Romeo and Juliet,*" he called.*

I laughed. "'O Romeo, Romeo, wherefore art thou, Romeo?' But I guess those would be my lines. Hold on. I'll be right down." I hurried down the stairs and opened the front door. "There you are," I said happily as I walked into his arms, which automatically pulled me close. "I was just wishing I had cell phone reception so I could call you, and there you were. Almost as if I'd wished you here."

"I always try to make your wishes come true," he murmured against my hair.

I realized that was true. When we were little, he always ran out to the playground and held my favorite swing until I could get there.

It was rare that there wasn't a bit of my favorite ice cream tucked up in the freezer. Pralines and cream.

"I thought I had to spend the night here because of the paint fumes at home?"

"You do, but I thought maybe I could spend the night with you?" He released his hug enough to kiss me. "I missed you."

"I missed you, too. And the lines for you would be 'But soft! What light through yonder window breaks? It is the east, and Juliet is the sun.'"

"I always saw you as the sun—bright and shining. People are drawn to you because of it, Addie. You bring out the best in them. You bring out the best in me."

I snuggled close. "That's not hard to do. You are so good that your best just shows through."

He shook his head. "I'm only at my best when you're around. I think there's a part of me that's missing. A part that you . . . I don't know. Fill in, if that makes sense."

"This is a very heavy conversation for a man who's sneaking into my room."

"Is that what I'm doing?" he asked.

"JoAnn's asleep and it's late at night, so yes, that's exactly what you're doing."

"I kind of like the idea of a clandestine rendezvous," he said.

I woke up with a start, remembering Gray's words as I curled around the blanket that smelled of him.

He'd been eloquent that night as he held me.

I realized my phone was buzzing in my pocket.

With fingers thick from sleep, I fumbled and finally got it out of my pocket. It was Peggy. "Honey, the nurse said the doctor will be making rounds soon. She thought you might want to be here."

"I do," I said groggily. "Thank you. I'll be there in just a few minutes."

I got up, refolded the blanket, and looked at this room. We'd had so many hopes and dreams for this baby.

Hearing that Gray had mourned him, too made me feel less alone.

I wished he'd mourned with me.

I thought about what Peggy had said, and I understood, but . . .

I wasn't sure it was enough.

I left the room as I'd found it and went back downstairs. I gathered my things from the hall and spotted Gray's Mercyhurst sweatshirt. He'd bought it back when Mercyhurst was still a college, not a university. The sweatshirt had a softness that only comes from years of wear and washing.

Without thinking, I pulled it on over my shirt. If I closed my eyes, I could almost believe that Gray was here, holding me.

I headed back to the hospital.

Before I went to the elevators, I stopped at the chapel. I didn't say anything; I simply stood for a moment, trusting that my intentions were heard. *Here I am*, I said in my head.

I turned to leave and saw Mark standing silently in the doorway.

"How is your husband?" he asked. "I was going to come up later and see you."

"He's holding his own. How's your father?"

He simply sighed. "He's the same as ever."

I reached out and patted his shoulder, remembering how others had done the same for me—given me some human contact. We both looked at each other, then nodded. He was right. Sometimes words were superfluous.

I went back to Gray's room. Smita was gone and Alice was back at her post. "I'm so glad you're here," I said.

"Your husband's doing fine," she assured me quickly. "On the other hand, his mother looks as if she might topple over at any moment."

"I'll try to get her to go home to sleep," I promised.

Peggy was pale and drawn as she looked up when I walked in.

It was as if getting here had given her something to do, but now that she was here, she felt as useless as I did.

"I can't stand to see him like this," she whispered.

I walked over, knelt by her chair, and took her hand. "He's doing better," I told her. "He's going to get through this."

"I don't know what I'd do without him."

I'd had the same thought. "Neither of us is going to have to find out." We stood for a few minutes next to him. He was on his back again.

I glanced at Peggy. "Why don't you go home and get some sleep."

She nodded. "You're staying the night?"

I leaned toward her and said, "I have a secret ace in the hole, so I'm pretty sure I am."

"Okay then." She started toward the door, then turned around. "He's been so alone since you left, Addie. It was as if he was only half there without you."

She turned and left before I could respond.

I wasn't sure how I would have responded, to be honest.

I moved back to the window and stood for the longest time, watching the world go by without Gray or me actively participating in it. Cars drove past the hospital on their way home from work. Giant yellow school buses as well.

People milled about on the sidewalks outside Gray's window.

People walked by with intent.

"Gray," I said, talking to Gray without looking at him. If I didn't look, I could pretend away the wires and tubes. I could pretend that we were sitting in the living room on the couch together. "It's gotten cold out in the last couple of days. But now it looks cold as well. There are dark black clouds out over the lake."

I thought about the ice cream in the freezer. "But it's never a bad time for ice cream," I murmured more to myself than to Gray.

"It looks like it wants to snow. It's too early, but then again this is Erie," I said. "You can never say it's too early or too late for snow. You know what they say, if you don't like the weather, just wait until tomorrow."

I stared outside for a few more moments, then said, "I love the snow. But you know that. Of course you know that.

"Do you remember when your mom would drive us to Four Mile Creek and that giant sledding hill that led down to it?"

Off Route 8, down Horseshoe Drive, around the bend, and up the slight incline. "The hill was tucked away. If you didn't know it was there, you'd never know it was one of the most amazing sled-riding hills ever. How did you ever find it? I don't remember."

I couldn't remember that, and I couldn't remember a time that Gray wasn't Gray. I couldn't remember a time when I called him Graham. I couldn't remember a time when he had a father at home.

How many memories do we forgot?

How many memories do we simply rewrite?

How many of our memories are truly of an actual event and how many did we rewrite simply by the telling of them? Until they became a memory of a story, more than of an actual event.

I thought my memory of that hill was true.

We'd gone out a few times every season. "I remember how the snow smelled—cold and white. Like peppermint, in my mind. Most of the time, the creek would be frozen, so if we had a good run on the sled, we'd shoot across to the opposite bank."

The creek was shallow in the best of times, so even if it wasn't frozen the worst we'd get was a little wet. "But we never knew for sure until our first run down. I guess we could have walked down to check, but we never did."

I could see it so clearly. "I remember I had my hair in braids because they froze and slapped at my cheeks as we went down that hill for an hour. We thought the creek was frozen, and we'd both shot to the far side of it repeatedly. But then we went down one time and must have veered a bit from our normal path. You jumped off before we hit the creek, but I didn't. I could hear the ice crack and I fell into the water, sled and all. It wasn't deep, but I was soaked."

Hitting the water had been a shock. For a moment I'd just sat there, then Gray had pulled me out.

"I remember you seemed so mad as we trudged up the hill. You dragged the sled with one arm and held my hand, pulling me up faster with your other hand.

"But when we got to the car, you finally looked at me, and I realized you weren't mad. You were worried I'd get sick from being wet in that kind of cold."

He'd tucked me into the front seat, as if I were an invalid and unable to seat myself.

"You put me in the front seat next to your mom and made her crank the heat up. When we got back to your house, your mom made me take a hot shower, and then gave me some of your sweats and your shirt to wear."

I hugged the sweatshirt I'd brought with me. "I knew they were clean because I could smell the fabric softener. But I swear I could smell you, too. It was the first time I ever wore your clothes."

I looked down at the age-softened sweatshirt. "When I moved out, I took one of your sweaters. That ratty gray one I always complained about. I wear it at night because it's the only way I can sleep—wrapped in your sweater, pretending it's your arms.

"Gray, it's been months since I walked out the door, and even with your sweater, I don't think I've slept one night through. I dream you're holding me and then I wake up and find you're not there. I dream I'm rocking our son, and I wake up and realize he died. He never drew a first breath.

"In my dreams, he smiles at me. His chubby fingers play with my hair as I rock him. I know that I'm really remembering a moment with Joey and mixing it up with dreams for our baby. I know it's another memory that my mind's rewritten, but for a few minutes I can believe the memory is of our son. Gray, sometimes those dream moments with him and with you are so real. Sometimes I think if I could just stay asleep with the two of you, I could be totally content."

I looked at Gray, who for all intents and purposes was sleeping.

"Come back to me," I said. "I'm not just talking about this." I waved at the machines and wires. "I'm talking about us. I might have left the house, but I feel as if you left me the moment we lost our son."

I picked up the swan.

"I don't want to lose you," I admitted. I set the swan down. I picked up the photo. How had the two kids in that picture grown so far apart?

All those happier moments I'd remembered in the last two days . . . how had I forgotten them? If it weren't for Gray's illness, would my mind have written over all of them, forever obscuring them? Would our worst moments have supplanted the best?

I set the picture down, but it wobbled and fell with a loud clatter to the tile floor. The glass shattered.

Alice popped her head into the room. "Is everything okay?"

I nodded. "I knocked our picture over."

"I love that photo," she said as she got the garbage can and came over to help me. "You both looked so young and happy."

"We were." I dropped glass into the can with her and then picked up the picture itself. There was something behind that high school picture of us. Without the glass, I could see a small lump. I popped open the back of the frame.

Our first sonogram picture of the baby. A picture when he was alive and we were still filled with our hopes and dreams for him.

There was writing on the back of it. I recognized Gray's firm hand. *Timothy Hunter Grayson.*

My breath caught. Alice said, "Addie, are you okay?"

I couldn't answer her because my silent sobs left me mute.

Gray had kept a picture of us, and of our son, on his desk.

He hadn't forgotten the baby or me.

Peggy had said as much, but this was a tangible sign.

"Addie?" Alice repeated.

I nodded. "I'm fine. It's just that Gray just told me what I'd wanted to hear months ago."

Peggy and Ash had both tried to say as much, but I needed to hear Gray tell me. And without saying a word, he had.

He'd told me that he loved me and that he'd loved our son.

Mark had been right.

Sometimes words weren't necessary.

As Gray lay there silent and sleeping, I'd heard the words I'd been waiting to hear all these months.

Chapter Thirteen

The doctor finally made her rounds. I'll confess, when she started talking in medical terms, all my frustrations bubbled over. Rather than waiting for Alice to translate, I said, "Could you put that in English?"

Before she could say it was English, I said, "The type of English non-doctors use?"

She had the grace to look chagrined and started again.

It was easier to focus now than it had been in the ER. Maybe my initial shock was wearing off.

She said if Gray made it through the night with no significant changes in his vitals, they'd withdraw the medication in the morning and allow him to wake up. She talked again about rehabilitation and a less stressful lifestyle for Gray.

I thought I'd be relieved to hear he was waking up, but instead I felt nervous.

Nervous that Gray would wake up and his blood pressure would spike.

Nervous that his stent would fail.

Nervous that I'd lose him all over again.

Nervous that he wouldn't be willing to make the lifestyle changes the doctor spoke of.

Nervous that despite everything, we wouldn't find our way back to the way we used to be.

"Thank you," I told the doctor.

"He's lucky to have you," she said.

I didn't know how to respond to that because he hadn't had me in a long time.

I just said, "Thank you."

She left and I turned back to Gray. "You have to take care of yourself," I whispered.

I couldn't lose him, not when I felt I was finally finding him again. The mangled envelope sat on the nightstand next to our photo, the plastic swan, and the sonogram picture.

"Do you think we can go back?" I asked Gray.

He didn't answer, but I thought about Maude. I had my answer. We couldn't go back, but if we were lucky, we could start over.

I found myself pacing the room, willing time to move faster. After months of apart, I didn't want to waste any more time. I wanted to talk to Gray.

I wanted him to wake up.

I walked to the window and watched the cars that flew past the small swatch of street I could see. They were driven by people heading home to loved ones. People who might not be thinking about how lucky they were. People who flew past the hospital without a thought for all the people in here waiting.

The people who went by were people who weren't buckling under the weight of that waiting. They were moving and going. Once Gray woke up, we'd be moving, too. I just wondered in what direction we'd go.

I finally sat back down and placed my hand on Gray's fingertips, needing to feel a connection with him.

Alice came in and spied me. She nodded approvingly. "Do you need anything?"

"No, but thank you."

She bustled around Gray. I was used to this by now. I pulled back my hand, allowing her room as she checked his tubes and wires, studied his vitals, readjusted this and that as needed. Then rolled him again.

She nodded toward the sonogram. "Your baby?"

I felt tears gather in my eyes. "Yes. Timothy Hunter," I said, using his name for the first time to someone else. "We lost him. Last December."

She leaned over and took my hand. "I'm so sorry for your loss."

"Thank you." That was all I intended to say, but then I found myself blurting out, "Gray never told me he mourned our son, too."

Alice seemed to consider my statement for a moment. Finally she said, "Some people don't say things because they're trying to hide ugly truths about themselves. But some people don't say them because they can't find the right words. Working here I've learned there's no such thing as perfect. I encourage patients to muddle through it the best they can. Perfection is overrated. Sometimes just being there is enough. Sometimes just being loved is all that matters. I've had to learn that sometimes being imperfect is good enough." She smiled and gave a self-deprecating laugh. "That was a very Mark-ish thing to say. So on that very wise and sage note, I'll say good night."

She left the room and I looked at Gray. I ran my finger through his hair, smoothing it more because of a need to touch him than any unruliness.

"She's right," I whispered to my husband. "I don't need the words, I just need your love."

His chest rose and fell to the rhythm of the machine.

"Do you remember in fourth grade? You asked me to go bowling with you. My parents dropped me off at the bowling alley, and your mom stayed with us. She very sweetly brought a book and sat in the lounge. I remember how patient you were as you tried to teach me to bowl. You showed me the dots on the floor and helped me line up my ball with them.

"But the moment that stands out the most in my memory was when you stood behind me and showed me how to swing and release the ball. Your left arm wrapped around my waist, and your right hand helped me hold the ball. It was just a little thing—that first touch. Casual, on your part. And even though I can't remember what movie we saw after the prom, I remember that moment. My nine-year-old self was sure I could spend the rest of my life bowling with you.

"When we were done, your mom drove me home. You walked me to the door because she insisted. You said to her, *You don't make me walk any of my other friends to the door.*"

I remembered those words, too.

"*Friends.* That's when I realized that what I—in my girlish way—thought was a first date was simply two friends going out bowling. You thought of me as your friend. So I let go of my nine-year-old dreams and was your friend. Because even then I wanted to be with you, no matter what you called it. Come back to me, Gray. I'll be your friend or your girlfriend or your wife. I'd like to be all three. But no matter what, I just want to be in your life."

I admitted, "I've missed you. If we'd never taken our relationship further than friendship, I think I might have been content. But after we lost . . . Timothy." Gray had given our son a name and for that I would always be grateful. "When we lost Timothy it felt like I was losing you. I didn't understand," I admitted. "I tried again to plan a honeymoon. I thought if maybe we could get away, we could find ourselves again. I thought we could remember the way we used to be."

I remembered that last day, before I'd left . . .

I sat in the front window of JoAnn's cottage. The bay was still covered with ice and dotted with fishing shacks. Most of the fishermen were safely tucked up inside, but on occasion, we'd see one walking to or from his winter getaway.

Soon the ice would start to melt and the shacks would be replaced by boats.

"We should do this more often," I said. "It's beautiful here any time of the year. I don't think I realized how winter's starkness had its own attraction. Maybe the fact that spring will be here soon amplifies the beauty."

I wasn't looking forward to spring. The winter bleakness matched my mood.

"The baby hasn't slept in days, so leaving Harmon with the kids . . ." She stopped. "I'm sorry."

"You can talk about the boys. They're a comfort to me."

Joey was a reminder of the son I'd lost. At first it had been hard, but now, holding him helped.

"I'm glad," she said. "But about this surprise. You've warned Gray against things like this."

"We need this," I said again. I needed my husband and he'd never felt so far away. "I didn't finalize anything. But Gray has got to know how much we need this. And the third time has to be the charm," I told JoAnn. I worked at infusing some enthusiasm into my voice because I knew she'd been worried about me.

For the first few weeks everyone had walked around on eggshells. Most didn't know what to say after I lost the baby. Some were embarrassed when they assumed I had a newborn at home and I had to explain.

Empathetic, or embarrassed, their concern for me written in their expressions.

The only person who wasn't concerned was the only person who might have truly understood what I was going through—Gray.

He'd shut the door to the baby's room at the house. He never mentioned the baby. He never mourned for him. It was as if he was pretending we'd never almost had a son.

So I put on a brave face every morning and tried to pretend that I was all right.

Eventually everyone seemed to buy it, except JoAnn.

"Addie" was all she said.

I smiled at JoAnn. "We need this. He'll see that."

She smiled, but I could see her skepticism. I didn't blame her. I didn't say it, but I had my doubts as well.

"JoAnn was right. Trying again for a honeymoon was not going to help us. I think I knew that from the start. But if you said no to going away with me, I had a reason to leave. A justification."

When I thought back to that day I could almost feel the white-hot glow of my anger. I'd been so angry. "I think all that anger was a way to cover up the pain. As long as I could stay angry . . ." I let the sentence fade away.

"I remember looking back at the house when I left that last time."

I'd kissed him good-bye and walked out of the house. I remember taking one last look back at the place I had thought I'd live forever with the man I loved. I'd pictured starting a family there and building a lifetime of memories.

"I remember looking back at the house and thinking it was time to build my memories somewhere else. I was wrong. You were and are a part of every memory. More than that, I want you to be part of my future—my future memories."

The anger was gone. And while I'd never get over losing my child, I could pick myself up and move on.

"I'm so sorry, Gray. I gave up and left. I was so hurt and I felt like you left me, but you hadn't." I held the sonogram photo now instead of the divorce papers.

I brushed the image of our son, set it down, and picked up the picture of me and Gray. "We were so happy."

We'd been full of such hopes and dreams.

"I'm sorry I walked away. I should have stayed and fought. I could try to excuse myself by saying I was destroyed and didn't have the wherewithal, but it would be just that, an excuse."

I knew that under all my anger and excuses, there was one ugly reason why I'd left. "I needed someone to blame and I blamed you. I knew you didn't want a baby right then and it was easy to blame you for his loss. That wasn't fair. I'm sorry, Gray."

I held the picture close.

I let go of the pain of Timothy. I'd always miss the child I'd dreamed he'd be, but I could let go of the unremitting pain.

"But I won't let go of you—of us. I've proven I can live without you, but since we've been here, I've realized that my life is only a half life without you in it. I could manage, but I want more than just managing. I want you. I need you, Gray. I'm sorry, and I hope when you wake up, you'll give us another try."

He looked so calm and peaceful. I no longer saw the wires and tubes. I just saw Gray, the man I loved.

The man I'd always loved, even if I'd forgotten for a time.

"Come back to me," I whispered. "Please come back to me."

Chapter Fourteen

I woke with a start. For a moment, I was confused, but suddenly the last few days came rushing back. I opened my eyes and saw Alice bustling around in the room.

"Sorry," she said when she saw I was awake. "I'll be leaving soon and wanted to do one more check before the next shift arrives."

"It's no problem." I sat up slowly. Somehow I'd held on to the picture as I slept. I set it on the stand, next to the envelope, and stretched. I was stiff from sleeping in an awkward position. There was enough light out to let me know I'd slept most of the night.

"You were exhausted," Alice said. "I'd say go home and grab a shower, but the doctor will be making rounds soon. You should stay for that. But I can find you some coffee if you'd like and put an order in for a breakfast."

I nodded. "Thank you. How does everything look?"

She smiled. "Good. He's stabilized nicely."

"So do you think they'll wake him up today?" I asked.

Alice never had a chance to answer. The doctor came in as I asked the question.

She looked at Gray, looked at Gray's chart, and then nodded to Alice.

The doctor turned to me and said, "Your husband has responded nicely to treatment, so we're going to wake him today."

"Are you sure?" I asked, nervous again. Not nervous about what would happen to us, but nervous for him. What if they woke him up and that stent gave out? What if I lost him for good and never got to apologize? What if . . .

"His blood pressure has stabilized," she answered, as if that said everything. It didn't. But she'd set her course and said, "Alice?"

Alice started fiddling with Gray's IV.

"How does this work?" I asked, dividing my attention between the doctor and Alice.

"We'll simply stop the medication that's been keeping him sedated. It's fast acting, so he'll wake up quickly. Once we're sure he's breathing on his own, we'll take out his breathing tube. Recuperating from the surgery will take some time and there will be pain, but we can manage that. I'll put him on morphine and he'll have a PCA." She must have seen my confusion and added, "A machine. He can administer the pain medication when he needs it. He'll be groggy from it."

I couldn't help but ask, "But he's out of the woods?"

The doctor smiled and nodded. "I'd say his prognosis is very good at this point. If he's willing to make a few lifestyle changes, he should have a long, ordinary life."

I knew she was saying that he'd be able to live a fairly normal life. Some people might want to insist on extraordinary, but ordinary sounded just fine to me.

Alice moved back and I stepped up and put my hand over Gray's fingertips again as his eyelids fluttered.

"Mr. Grayson, can you open your eyes?" the doctor asked.

Slowly, he opened his eyes and blinked rapidly as if trying to clear something from them. He seemed confused.

"I'm here, Gray," I said.

He looked at me and tried to talk.

"Mr. Grayson," the doctor said, "we've got a tube down your throat that's been helping you breathe. If you give us a minute, we'll see what we can do about removing it. Just be calm and try to breathe normally." The doctor moved toward the head of his bed. "Alice?"

Alice fiddled with a dial and both she and the doctor turned their attention to monitors. I simply watched Gray.

"I'm so glad you're back with me," I whispered. "I have so much I need to say to you. I'm sorry. I'm sorry for everything."

I let Alice and the doctor do their thing and kept focused on Gray. He seemed more alert. He moved his hand, disregarding the IV, and held mine tight.

I'm not sure how long we sat like that. To see him, to have him alert and aware of me was all that mattered.

Finally the doctor was satisfied with whatever she was seeing. She said, "We're going to remove your breathing tube, Mr. Grayson. I need you to blow out, as if you're blowing up a balloon."

He gripped my hand as she removed the tape that had held the tube in place, then she took it in hand and said, "Now, Mr. Grayson."

Within seconds the tube was out.

Gray coughed hard and then winced.

The doctor saw his expression and said, "You're probably going to have a sore throat for a time. That's perfectly normal."

Gray nodded.

"Do you know where you are, Mr. Grayson?" the doctor asked.

He looked around and then nodded. "The hospital." His voice was raspy.

"Yes," she said, nodding and smiling as if he'd passed a test. "You had an aortic dissection type A. Basically a tear in your aorta. You had open-heart surgery and you've been sedated. Alice is going to start some medication that will help with the pain."

Gray nodded as the doctor continued to explain his condition, but his eyes were on me. He gripped my hand harder, as if afraid I'd disappear.

"I'm not going anywhere," I assured him softly.

The doctor seemed to be winding down. ". . . and you'll have a few restrictions, Mr. Grayson. I don't think you'll be running any marathons, but you should go on to make a complete recovery and have a normal life."

"Thank you," he said.

The doctor left the room and Alice started a new small bag of medication on the pole, next to Gray's IV fluid. She ran the line for it through another machine and handed him a button. "If the pain gets to be too much, you can push this button and the machine will give you more medication."

"He can't overdose?" I asked. The doctor had said morphine and I knew that was a strong drug.

Alice shook her head. "No, the machine is designed to prevent that."

She helped Gray move the head of the bed to a slightly elevated position. She checked and rechecked his vitals.

She got him ice chips and promised something more substantial soon.

I liked Alice, but neither of us paid much attention to her.

Maybe she'd watched long enough, or maybe she sensed that Gray wanted to say something and wouldn't in front of her. Either way, she finally said, "I think you're fine, Mr. Grayson. I'll be just out at my station."

"Thank you," he said again.

She left and still Gray didn't say anything to me.

"Can I get you something?" I finally asked.

"You can come closer." He spoke softly, as if anything more than a whisper hurt.

I sat on the edge of the bed, right next to his head. I brushed my fingertips against his cheek and he leaned into them.

"How long has it been?" he asked.

"A couple of days. Your mom's here. I sent her home for some rest overnight. She'll be here soon, but I should let her know you're awake. And Ash and JoAnn. I'll text her first, then—"

"In a minute," he said. I nodded, understanding. I wasn't ready to share him with anyone else yet. Not even Peggy.

"Your mom moved heaven and earth to get back to Erie," I told him.

"Her cruise," he said, remembering.

"Yes. They told her it would be faster to stay on the boat, but she chartered a small plane to take her from the island to Florida, then she caught a commercial plane home. She spent money from the account you set up for her. She feels bad about that, but she was thankful to have it."

He shook his head and winced again. I wasn't sure if his neck was as stiff as mine, or if his chest hurt. Either way, I said, "You can push the button, Gray."

"No. Not yet. I want to talk to you," he said. In addition to the gravel in his voice, I heard worry.

"I'm not going anywhere. I'm here, I promise. I'll let everyone know you're awake and try to get some sleep myself." I threw that last bit in because I suspected thinking I needed some rest might be enough to prompt Gray to take the medicine.

"You'll be here when I wake up?" he asked.

"I promise."

He nodded and pushed the button. I could see him visibly relax as the medication did its job and slowly his eyes closed. His grip on my hand loosened, but he didn't let go.

I pulled my phone from my pocket and texted Peggy, then Ash and JoAnn.

I must have dozed off as well because I awoke with a start to find Peggy standing by the bed.

"He looks so much better," she said.

I looked at him and nodded. "He's just sleeping now. He's on heavy-duty pain medication, but he's okay. You can come in and wait for him to wake up."

She shook her head. "He needs you now. He's always needed you, Addie. Just keep me updated." She hugged me.

I hugged her back. Not just some social hug, but I unashamedly clung to her. I realized I was crying again.

"Shh," she said. "He's okay."

"We almost lost him," I said between my tears. "What if—"

"No," she interrupted. "We're not going to play that game. The fact of the matter is, he's here. My son is a stubborn man and he's strong. He'll do what needs to be done."

I nodded and wiped my eyes. "You're right."

"Keep me posted," she said. She kissed his forehead and left.

I alternated between standing and staring out the window, and sitting and staring at Gray.

The nurse brought me food, but I moved it around more than ate it.

Gray finally stirred again and I pushed the tray aside, practically untouched. "Addie?" he called.

"I'm here. I didn't leave," I said.

He winced again and I knew he was in pain.

"Take some more pain medicine, Gray. Your mom was here. She'll be back. And I talked to Ash and JoAnn. Jo says as soon as you're able, she'll visit. And if you protest, I'm supposed to remind you that as a friend you should say yes so she can leave the kids with Harmon and have a few minutes to herself."

I smiled. "I'm supposed to assure you that her visit is more about her than you."

Despite his discomfort, he smiled. "Her kids . . ."

I knew what he was thinking and asking. "It's all good. Snuggling with Joey helped me. There's no snuggling Wills anymore. He's too big for that."

"We need to talk," Gray managed.

"Later. Get some more rest. I'm not going anywhere. We have a lot to talk about, but all you need to know right now is I'm sorry and I love you."

"Love you, too," he said.

He grimaced, so I knew the pain was getting worse. "Push the button, Gray."

He finally did, and I watched as his expression eased and he fell back to sleep.

That became our rhythm for the rest of the day. He'd wake up, we'd talk about inconsequential things, the pain would increase, and he'd go back to sleep. Slowly we added layers onto the routine.

Ice chips.

Then sips of water.

By that evening, he had some broth.

I didn't pick up the poor envelope. I left it on the stand, next to the picture, the sonogram, and swan.

As he slept, I alternated between looking at the items on the nightstand, and looking at him.

Every time his chest rose, then fell, I felt it was a victory.

Every time he stirred, or coughed, we were closer to recovery.

Every moment that went by, I treasured.

Each time he woke up he was a little more alert and stayed awake a little longer before he pressed the button for more pain medication.

When he was ready, I had so much I wanted to tell him.

There was so much he needed to know.

And all of it could be said succinctly in just three words.

I love you.

And maybe the three words that Mark said mattered, too. *Here I am.* I leaned close to Gray, who was sleeping again, and I whispered both. "Here I am. I love you."

I thought I saw him smile.

The next morning I woke with a start. I sat up and caught my hand in the bed's railing. I swore softly as I shook it. I'm not sure why I thought shaking it would help . . . it didn't. So I simply rubbed it with my other hand.

Then I realized that Gray was looking at me. "Have you been here the whole time?"

I studied him. He wasn't sitting straight up, but he was definitely more vertical than horizontal. His brown eyes looked sharp and clear. He still looked drawn, but he looked more like himself.

He stared at me expectantly and I realized he'd asked a question. "Yes, I've been here. Except for a couple of trips home for showers and changes of clothes."

He didn't say anything; he simply reached for the hand I'd banged. He held it with one hand, and stroked the area above my wrist with the other, as if he sensed just where it hurt.

Gradually his movements slowed, then stopped altogether. I realized he'd fallen back to sleep.

He looked peaceful.

Gray had always been many things. Peaceful wasn't one of them.

He was driven. Ambitious. Loyal. And loving.

He squeezed my hand, as if to be sure it was still present. He opened his eyes again.

"I'm here," I said softly. "Gray, I want you to know that I'm sorry, I—"

He interrupted my apology. "I love you. When I collapsed, all I could think about was that I hadn't said those words enough. I love you, Addie. I should have told you a lot of things, but I should have said those words the most. I should have told you every day."

I thought about the divorce papers. How had I thought I could go through with it? "I love you, too. I always have."

He turned toward me and winced.

"Gray, this all can wait until later." I didn't want to stress him. "I'm here, I love you, and I'm sorry for everything. The rest is all beside the point."

He shook his head. "No, it's not. The rest of it matters. I heard you. Well, bits of things. Maybe some of it was a dream. But I think some of it was real. I heard Mom tell you . . ." His voice broke and he paused a moment.

"It's all right," I said. "You don't need to now."

After months of wanting nothing more than for him to open up and share with me, it was just enough that he was here. He was awake.

I'd blamed him, but I knew in my heart that I'd made him my whipping boy. "I'm sorry," I said again. "We don't need to say any more than that."

He shook his head. "I heard Mom tell you about after the baby. Addie, I should have told you. I wanted him more than you'll ever know. I should have said that. I should have cried with you. I didn't realize . . ." He sighed. "I wanted to be strong for you."

"I know that now, Gray. For a long time, I blamed everything on you. I think I needed someone to blame, and you've always been so close to me. It made you an easy target. But sitting here, I realized that we were both lost and hurting. And rather than reaching for each other, we both pulled away."

I felt the need to be honest, to say the words. I'd realized something without even realizing I was realizing it. "When I tried to book that one last trip for us, I think I knew you'd say no. It gave me an excuse. I said you pulled away and wouldn't talk to me. I stoked my anger at you. Don't you see? All this wasn't you pulling away or saying the wrong thing. It wasn't the honeymoon we didn't take. It was me. I did this. I was broken and you couldn't put me back together. I blamed you for that. And being angry with you was so much easier than being angry with myself. This was my fault. And I'm sorry for that."

He closed his eyes again. I couldn't tell if he'd fallen asleep again or was simply finding this conversation too taxing. "We can talk about all this later, Gray. I love you and I'm here for as long as you want me to be. All that matters now is getting you well," I whispered.

He shook his head. "I will always want you, Addie. But I need to say . . . I need to say all the things I should have said before. I tried to tell you, but everything I said came out wrong."

Maybe it's for the best.

Those words had haunted me. They'd fueled my anger and made me feel justified blaming Gray. Blaming him for something that couldn't have been his fault any more than it was mine.

I glanced at the sonogram. Timothy Hunter Grayson.

I knew that Gray hadn't meant those other words. He'd said everything he needed to say when he'd named our son.

As if he read my thoughts, he said, "I said something about it being for the best. I know that hurt you. But what I meant . . . I couldn't stand the thought of our son suffering. I know afterward the tests said there was nothing genetically wrong, but . . . I didn't mean . . ."

"I know you didn't," I told him. "I was so angry and that anger needed a target. But I know you didn't mean that."

I remembered a promise I'd made him right after we started dating in college. We were sitting in the library when Candy, Gray's prom date all those years ago, walked by. She stopped and chatted a few minutes, then left. And Gray said . . .

ꟸ ꟸ ꟸ

"She's still pretty."

"Oh, really?" I asked, half teasing, half miffed. I knew that Candy was pretty, but I didn't want Gray to notice it, or even worse, comment on it.

"Yes," he said.

I was always amazed by the cues he missed. I mean, he could notice Candy's prettiness, but not my annoyance?

I knew that being annoyed was crazy and not the least bit rational. But I couldn't seem to stop myself.

He looked at me and I could see it register that I didn't necessarily like him talking about other girls being pretty. "Sorry."

"No, you're right, she's always been pretty," I said, trying to tamp down my annoyance.

No. Not annoyance. Jealousy. I was jealous of Candy. And I didn't like feeling that way.

Gray shook his head. "Candy's always been pretty, but she's always known it."

I really wanted this conversation to end, so I simply said, "Okay."

"No, it's not okay," he insisted with a sigh. "I'm making a mess of this. Candy's pretty and knows it. You're pretty and don't know it. That's part of your . . ." He paused.

"Charm?" I supplied. I'm not sure about the pretty part, but I was charmed.

"Yeah," he said. "Listen, Addie, I am . . ." He paused again, searching for the right word.

I couldn't help fill it in this time, so I just waited.

"Socially awkward," he finally said. "Remember Susie? She told me that I was socially awkward." He glanced at me quickly, as if to check that I wasn't going to get all green-eyed about that.

"She was wrong," I said with a smile.

Jealousy wasn't a game I normally played. I didn't like the feeling and resolved to try to avoid it in the future.

"Listen," he said. "In my head my compliments are just that—compliments. But somewhere between my head and my mouth they can turn into something else entirely."

"You do okay," I assured him. "After all, you did say I was pretty."

"You see, I goofed that up, too. Adeline Frasier, you are more than just pretty. To me you're the most beautiful woman in the world."

"Now that was pretty much perfect," I said and kissed him.

When the kiss ended he said, "Maybe when I mess up the next time, you should just ask me what I really meant."

"I should ask what it sounded like in your head before it got to your mouth?" I teased.

He looked relieved and nodded. "Yes."

⁂

"I forgot to ask you what you meant," I said. "All those years ago in college, you told me that sometimes you said things all wrong, and I promised to ask what you really meant. I didn't. I'm sorry."

"I thought I was being strong for you, but you didn't need my strength, you just needed me to share the grief with you. You needed me to be present." He closed his eyes and said, "I had so many plans for him, you know. I was going to be the father I never had. Like your dad. Like my mom, for that matter. My mom was the best mother, but she also managed to be the best father. I was going to show up at his games, and read to him. I thought that when he was old enough, we'd surprise him with a trip to Disney World. I mean, really surprise him. Not tell him until the morning, as we left for the airport. I'd researched it. And . . ."

He shook his head and opened his eyes.

I realized that he had tears in them.

Those tears were my undoing. I started to cry as well. I cried for Timothy Hunter. I cried because I'd lost Gray long before I'd almost lost him to his illness.

"I'd give up the business and all my plans for a chance to be all that for him. I will never get over losing him," he said.

"And all the dreams that died with him," I said, understanding.

He nodded. "Addie, I'll be or do whatever you need if you'll give me another chance. We can go back—"

I thought about Maude, meeting Bertie at the Piggly Wiggly in Waunakee, Wisconsin. "We can't go back, but we can make a new start."

Maude, James, Harriet, Siobhan, and Mark—I might never know some of their last names or what they did for a living, but they'd all made a profound impact on me.

"I talked to other people who were waiting for their loved ones while I was waiting for you. They shared a lot of their happy moments.

"Here I am, Gray, and here I'm going to stay—with you. I love you. We never forgot our love, but we forgot to be there for each other." I shrugged. "I'm not sure that makes sense to you."

It made sense to me. I squeezed his hand again. "The day I came to your office, I'd thought that I wanted to shake you and make you remember the way we used to be, but I had it all wrong. It wasn't just you, it was me. I got stuck on that one horrible moment and forgot the hundreds of other moments. The better moments. The wonderful moments. Even the mundane moments. I forgot them all. All I could remember was losing the baby and then feeling as though I'd lost you as well."

"And now?" he asked.

"While you were sleeping I fell in love with you again. Or maybe I just remembered that I never stopped loving you." Like one of those digital picture frames, the moments tumbled over each other in my mind. "Right now, I can see us in a classroom. We had to have been very young because I was at a desk where the seat wasn't attached. You were leaning over me, explaining something. I don't remember what, but I do remember you saying, *Just take your time, you'll get it. You'll figure it out.*"

He'd trusted me to figure it out then. "Well, I figured it out now. I never stopped loving you, but while you were sleeping, I fell in love with you all over again."

"I love you," he said, then closed his eyes. And slowly his breathing changed. I realized he'd fallen asleep again.

If this were a movie, it might seem anticlimactic, but for me, it was fine. I loved him. He loved me. That was enough.

I sat back down, and when Alice stuck her head into the room, I held a finger to my lips to let her know he was sleeping.

She tiptoed in, checked on him, then nodded and tiptoed out.

I stood and looked out the window. The sky was a bright blue today with big, fluffy fall clouds. Sometime soon, we'd leave this hospital and go home.

I glanced back at the man I loved. He was still sleeping. A small smile played across his lips. I wondered what he was dreaming about.

For the next couple of hours, we had snippets of conversations. It was as if Gray had suddenly discovered all the words he'd never said.

Every time he woke up, he looked for me.

I saw his fear that I'd left and his relief each time he realized I hadn't gone anywhere.

"After you moved into JoAnn's," he said, "I used to ride the elevator every morning and watch as the bay came into view. You were my first thought. And though I knew I couldn't see you, I felt you. All day, I used to stare out my window looking at the bay, wishing I could see you. Then at night, as I left the office, I'd watch the bay disappear from view and I would miss you even more."

He'd fallen asleep, and when he woke, he didn't miss a beat as he continued, "Sometimes, I didn't leave my office. I slept on the couch and spent the night staring at the lights on the edge of the bay, wondering if one of them was yours."

I didn't have a chance to respond before he dozed off again.

Smita came in this time.

"He keeps falling asleep. Is it the drugs?" I asked.

"He just had open-heart surgery and is taking some heavy-duty pain medication. He'll still be a bit loopy for a while." She looked at me. "It's normal. He's okay."

Those were the words I wanted to hear.

As Smita left, Gray squeezed my hand. "Do you know one of the things I missed the most while you were gone?"

I shook my head.

"Your singing," he said.

I managed a small smile. "Maybe I should call the doctor . . . you are obviously delusional."

"No, I mean it," he said. "You were always singing around the house. It seemed too quiet without that."

I had my own little playlist of songs that I sang without even thinking about it. I realized that I hadn't done much singing since I left Gray.

To be honest, I'm not sure that I'd done any.

And I realized at this moment I truly felt like singing again.

"Sometimes you'd catch me midsong and laugh," I said. "I think I sang all the more because I loved to hear that sound. You are a very serious person by nature." I smiled as I said the words.

Gray nodded his agreement, wearing a very serious expression, but then like a small ray of sunshine, I could see his smile lurking behind it. "There's one song I remembered you singing about a man who didn't have the words. I spent weeks listening to your iPod, trying to find it. And when I did, I think I listened to it—to the entire musical—a hundred times."

"Wait. You had my iPod? I couldn't find it when I moved."

"I found it under the table, but I didn't return it. When I missed you the most, I'd turn it on."

I reached out and ran my finger across his stubbled face. "Ash said you were listening to musicals and it freaked him out. Which song were you hunting for?"

"From *They're Playing Our Song*. I read the synopsis after I found it. I saw me in that main character. He had music and he understood the notes, but the words escaped him. I understand business. I know how to find the information I want, I know how to point the company in the direction I want it to go, but Ash, he's the one who gets the people. He makes it happen."

Gray closed his eyes and for a moment I thought he was going to fall asleep again, but instead he said, "I had the perfect life. Ash at work and you at home. I didn't even try to say the things I should have because I had you, and you always seemed to understand. Then you left and I couldn't figure out what I needed to say in order to get you back."

"I'm sorry, Gray. I never should have—" I stopped because he'd fallen asleep again. This time I waited, knowing he'd wake again and pick up our conversation.

I could wait, I realized. We didn't have to finish this now because we had time. The rest of our lives.

His eyes fluttered and he began to wake up. "I know I'll need you to help me find the words in the future, but sometimes the words need to be said. A partnership has to be able to change. I let you down because I pulled away and didn't say the words. You weren't asking for an opus."

"I didn't need—"

"You did. You need to hear me say *I love you* and, more than that, you needed to hear me say *I loved our son*. You needed me to say *I miss him and I will miss him for the rest of my life*. You needed to hear me say *lean on me and let me lean on you. We'll get through this together*. I let you down because rather than reaching for you, I turned away just like my father did. Only he made a clean break and left physically."

"I only need three words from you, Gray," I told him. "Three words and you standing by my side. I don't need you to be strong for me. I don't need you to save me. I just need you with me and—"

"I love you," he said.

"Those were the words," I assured him. "I love you, too."

He drifted off to sleep again.

I glanced at the nightstand. There was our picture from before we were a couple. The black plastic swan from the moment that changed us and we were a couple. And Timothy. They all belonged together. They all represented our journey to here.

One thing on that nightstand did not belong.

I reached for the smudged, mangled envelope that I'd carried throughout the ordeal. I got up, took it across the room, and dropped it in the garbage.

It landed with a very satisfying thump.

I went back to Gray and whispered as he slept. "Here I am." And most importantly, "I love you."

The next morning, Alice came into the room. She smiled when she saw we were both awake. "Have you had your breakfast yet?" she asked.

"Not yet," I said with little enthusiasm. The food was adequate, but . . . But. Each meal was edible, but everything was bland.

Her smile grew as she handed Gray a bag. "Have fun, you two," she called as she turned around and left the room.

"What on earth are you two up to?" I asked.

Gray didn't say anything as he handed me the bag.

I opened it up. Two small containers and two spoons were in the bag. "Breakfast?" I asked.

He nodded. "You know I believe in balanced breakfasts. There's dairy, and the nuts are protein . . ."

I popped the lid. "Pralines and cream," I said.

"It's never a bad time for ice cream," he repeated.

I took a bite and handed him his.

As we ate our ice cream and talked, I felt loved.

Two weeks later, when we went home, I finally opened the freezer.

Gray hadn't just bought a few half gallons. No. The freezer was full. Every shelf filled with almost every kind of ice cream I could imagine. And I heard so clearly what he was saying without words.

I heard his footsteps over the whir of the refrigerator. "Every time I went to the store, I bought a couple more," he admitted from behind me. "It made me feel better. It made me think of you."

I turned around, found my husband, and hugged him as I whispered, "I love you."

"I love you."

The words were sweeter than ice cream.

Epilogue

"To the co-owner of Harbor House," Gray said, lifting his wineglass.

I tapped mine to his and took a sip.

It was neither too sweet nor too dry.

It was a perfect blend. Rather like Gray and me. The thought made me smile.

"What?" Gray asked.

"I am happy," I said. Those three words summed up my feelings. "This is the honeymoon I always wanted."

I'd thrown a buffalo-plaid blanket over my shoulders and along with Gray's arm, I was warm enough.

I looked at Gray, who was looking toward the peninsula as the sun slipped behind it, leaving a blaze of orange and pink in its wake.

"I get it now," he said, more to himself than to me.

But I asked, "Get what?"

"Why you love sunsets so much. Every time I watch one now, I realize that it's the end of another day . . . another day I spent with you. That's a gift."

It was such an un-Gray-like thing to say, but I'd noticed that he'd said a lot of un-Gray-like things since we'd gotten back together. I tried not to take moments like this for granted.

I moved closer to him and draped the throw over his shoulder, too, as I snuggled under his arm. We watched the last of the color fall below the peninsula as well, leaving the evening stars in its wake.

I started to move, ready to go back inside, but Gray held me in place and turned so we were facing each other, the blanket still hanging over both our shoulders. He reached under it and into his pocket.

"This is for you," he said.

I opened the box, and inside was a round opal ring. "I gave you a ring when we got engaged. I gave you another one when we got married. And I wanted to give you something to celebrate us. The last year has been . . ."

He seemed to run out of words, but I remembered the promise I'd made so many years ago and listened to what he was trying to say. "It's been amazing," I filled in.

He nodded. "Yes. The girl at the jewelry store said opals are a stone that people don't buy for themselves. She said they're best given as a gift, and that in some folklore they're known as the *anchor of hope*. I liked that."

I slipped it on my right ring finger and it fit perfectly. I kissed him and said, "I like it, too."

"I thought this was the perfect gift to represent our anchors of hope."

My heart melted a little and I understood perfectly what he was trying to say.

"I've sort of bought you an early Christmas present, too," I said. "Sort of," I reiterated.

"Sort of?" he asked.

"Well, it's a big gift, and while I think you'll like it, I didn't want to commit to that kind of money without asking you. There's time to stop it if you want, but I don't think we should."

"Is it here?" he asked.

"Inside." We quietly opened the sliding glass door and walked back into the bedroom with the bed positioned so the first thing you'd see in the morning was the bay. As I entered the first thing I saw was our own personal anchor of hope.

I tossed the blanket on the chair and it landed on a rattle. The noise was sharp in the quiet room. I held my breath a moment, but there was no other sound.

I picked up the large manila envelope from my overnight bag and I handed it to Gray.

"Another honeymoon?" he asked quietly, smiling.

After he got out of the hospital, we'd talked about going to an island resort somewhere, but in the end, life got in the way of flying, so we'd come here, to Ferncliff. "Being with you is all the honeymoon I'll ever need. Plus, I don't think we could have gone anywhere in the world and found such lovely souvenirs."

I glanced at the bed where our *anchors* were still lying.

I knew that kind of stillness wouldn't last long.

Gray followed my look and kissed my forehead, then hesitantly opened the envelope, scanned the paper, and looked at me with questions in his eyes.

"It's the cottage next door," I explained, pointing to the ramshackle building to my right. "I think JoAnn stayed away this year in order to give us a regular escape from the real world. I feel like we've rediscovered us again down here. It's been a yearlong honeymoon."

We came almost every weekend that JoAnn wasn't using the house.

"I know they're busy with the boys' activities and they didn't use it much," I said. "But I think they'd have used it more if it weren't for us.

I've felt guilty, and when I heard the one next door was going on the market, I went over and talked to Mr. Laraby. If we buy it, he won't have to list it with an agent, so he'd give us a very fair deal. Then I went to the bank and here's what our payments would be."

"You want us to move here?" he asked.

"No. I want us to live on Willow Lane and keep coming down here for vacations—honeymoons. All of us. I'd like JoAnn and Harmon to bring their kids here, and our family would be next door. I like to think of years of all of us coming down here. The kids growing up together down here."

I glanced again at the king-size bed. The babies both slept soundly in the middle of it.

When Gray and I rediscovered each other, I thought that I had reached the pinnacle of happiness. Then when I'd found out I was pregnant, fear mixed with joy. Joy mixed with love. So much more love.

We'd clung to each other throughout the pregnancy, terrified we'd lose these babies, too, but not turning away from each other. No, we'd held on tight.

"I look at it as a lifetime of honeymoons," I said. "I want you to teach Maude Alice and Mark James to fish here. I want to buy a canoe when they're bigger, and row across the bay to the peninsula."

"And maybe lie on the deck and watch the sunset behind Presque Isle?" he asked.

I nodded. "Us. The four of us. We'll escape here for a day or a weekend. We'll shut out the world and just be us."

"It would be a lot of work," he said. "I was in Mr. Laraby's house that one time. It's got paneling."

"I don't care, but we can paint it if it bothers us." I could almost see us all working, the four of us smeared with paint as we laughed.

"His kitchen is ancient," Gray said.

"It's antique. I like antiques," I insisted. "Plus, JoAnn has a handyman who takes care of stuff at the store. I've never met a job that Darius couldn't do. I'm sure he'd help us out with anything that has to be fixed."

"I like the whole history of Ferncliff, and you're right, having JoAnn and Harmon as neighbors would be a bonus. And I really like the view here," he said slowly. I realized that rather than looking at the now-dark bay, he was looking at me.

I looked back at Gray. At the man I loved.

"Addie, thank you for the gift."

"Then you want the cottage?" I asked, checking that's what he meant.

"Yes. But the gift I was thinking of was you and our kids. And . . ." he hesitated.

"Those words are good enough, Gray. I love you, too," I assured him. "More than pickles."

"More than sunsets," he said in return.

"More than ice cream," I said.

Before Gray could add another *more than*, Maude stirred, which woke her brother up. I reached for her, and Gray picked up Mark.

I watched him holding our son and I remembered that day I planned on giving him those papers. I'd thought *I must have loved him once.*

I'd been right.

I had loved him once.

Then I loved him again.

And now I knew with certainty that I'd love him always.

Author's Note

February 2015

Dear Reader,

I think that good marriages tend to be built on two sets of three words. *Here I am* and *I love you*. I loved exploring how a couple could not only find true love once, but could rediscover it again.

I've loved and been married to the same man for years . . . wait, decades. And while I've never fallen *out* of love with him, I have fallen *in* love with him all over again many times.

I've talked about the "Easter eggs" I've hidden in my books before. They're bits of myself that work their way into every story. Some are big ones that most of my readers and friends might pick up on (my hometown, Erie, Pennsylvania, Mondays, and *Glee* are pretty blatant) and some are just special little references that only one other person gets.

They're Playing Our Song is a huge Easter egg . . . an homage to my love of Broadway. I'm pretty sure a lot of friends and readers will get that. But those references are something more individual, too.

I was a junior in high school when my mother and father went to New York City. Mom brought me back a pair of pajamas from Saks Fifth Avenue. I'd never heard of the store (sorry, Saks) and she was disappointed that I wasn't impressed by the tan box with the Saks name emblazoned on it. I still feel bad that I ruined her surprise.

But Mom brought me back an even better gift that day. She'd bought the album from the Broadway show they'd seen, *They're Playing Our Song*. Lucie Arnaz and Robert Klein played a lyricist and composer in it—she writes the words and he writes the melodies. Romance ensues. At the end of the show, they've broken up and Robert Klein's character sits in the hospital singing "Fill in the Words." He needs the heroine to find the words for him.

That song kept playing over and over in my head as I wrote this book. That idea of someone who can't find the words for himself inspired Gray. Gray loves, and loves completely, but he doesn't know how to tell Addie. He can't always put all his feelings into words. And sometimes when he does find the words, they come out wrong. I think that everyone has experienced those moments when what you're trying to say doesn't just come out wrong, it comes out *so* wrong.

The story was written from Addie's point of view . . . it was told in *her words*. That made sense to me and to the story. But through Addie's words, Gray finds his. They both suffer under the weight of their waiting and the weight of their loss, but in the end they both realize that the most important words are *I love you*. Everything else builds from them.

I hope you enjoyed the story. And for those of you who read *Carry Her Heart*, you'll see that Siobhan had a cameo in this book. Her story is in the works . . . so you'll get to go back and visit with Ned and Pip.

I want to thank you all for your unbelievable support. Thank you for the letters, the Twitter and Facebook posts. Just thank you!

And a special thanks to JoAnn Ross and Kelli Martin. JoAnn read *Just One Thing* and along with Kelli, my editor, said, "More like that, Holly." Thanks to them both for the encouragement.

And a special thanks to my mom. I might not have known what Saks Fifth Avenue was, but, like Gray, I played that album hundreds of times! My kids all know the music to that show, too. It was one of the reasons I fell in love with Broadway . . . and that's a gift that's stayed with me, long after the pajamas wore out.

Holly

About the Author

Award-winning author Holly Jacobs has sold over two million books worldwide. The first novel in her Everything But . . . series, *Everything But a Groom*, was named one of 2008's Best Romances by *Booklist*, and her books have been honored with countless other accolades.

Holly has a wide range of interests, from her love for writing to gardening and even basket weaving. She has delivered more than sixty author workshops and keynote speeches across the country. She lives in Erie, Pennsylvania, with her family and her dogs. She frequently sets stories in and around her hometown.

Made in the USA
Monee, IL
07 September 2026

62521460R00119